C000134694

A BAD DEATH

DAVID MARK

PRAISE FOR DAVID MARK

'Dark, compelling crime writing of the highest order' *Daily Mail*

'Brilliant' *The Sun*

'Exceptional... Mark is writing at the top of his game.' *Publishers Weekly*

'A wonderfully descriptive writer' *Peter James*

'A class act. Utterly original and spine chillingly good, when it comes to crime fiction, David Mark is in the premier league." *Abir Mukherjee, author of A Rising Man*

'One of the most imaginative crime writers in the business, David Mark knows how to tell a good story - usually one that will invoke feelings of extreme horror and awe... in a good way, of course!' *S J I Holliday, author of The Lingering*

'Aector McAvoy, Mark's gentle giant, is one of the most fascinating, layered characters in British crime fiction. Mark is an outstanding writer.' *M W Craven*

'Masterful' *Michael Ridpath*

'A true original' *Mick Herron*

'To call Mark's novels police procedurals is like calling the Mona Lisa a pretty painting.' *Kirkus Reviews*

'Mark writes bad beautifully' *Peter May*

OTHER NOVELS BY DAVID MARK

'Every man is guilty of the good he did not do.'

Voltaire

PROLOGUE

THEN

The Humber Bridge Country Park.
Five miles from Hull, East Yorkshire.

The gale pulls at the tails of the dancing garrotte, yanking it tighter around the trunk of the half-dead sycamore. It becomes a ligature: a noose of blue and white police tape. It chews through the rotten bark and into the living flesh of the tree; throttling this throat of pale wood.

This is the place.

The place where the girl said he had hurt her.

The place where she *lied*.

Owen forces himself to look away. Still, he can visualize the tightening knot; the bubbles of oozing sap. He hides his face with his hand, closing his eyes, pushing back the memory before it can rise to the surface. He's cursed with a good imagination. Can picture himself, all too easily, doing the things they claim he did. He can't stand to see it all again.

Can't stand to look upon himself, squeezing the life out of her: trousers around his ankles and her trainers leaving muddy footprints on his thighs.

Breathless, his fingers making fists, he snatches a glance his watch, wiping rain from its face and from his own. Jerks his head skywards. Damp leaves and rotten branches form a ragged canopy over this sparse patch of woodland. The ground is too rocky for the trees to thrive. Beyond, the sky is all ripped tissue and hard slate.

He looks down.

Amid the mulch of timber and twigs, there is evidence that this place has seen violence. Polythene evidence bags. The page of a note-book, littered with crossings-out. The prints of size-ten shoes, forming fish-shaped hollows in the mud. They took pictures. Maybe one of the men and women in white suits asked why they couldn't find anything. More likely they didn't care.

A sound, gunshot-sharp, jerking him back to the sheer raw Hell of this here, this place, this *now*.

THROUGH THE TREES comes a charcoal figure: skinny and small, as if made of twists of tarred, knotted rope. He's hunched up inside a dirty, camel-coloured raincoat and the thin cigar at his lips is unlit. He sucks on it anyway, turning the stub into a mulch of tobacco, brown paper and spit.

"Fucking hell, Owen," shouts Tony, as his feet slurp at the path. "This is bloody horrible. Where you planning for the summer? Self-catering in Helmand?"

Owen feels as though he is seeing him for the first time.

Tony has never been attractive. He's a rat in a raincoat; all bad skin and yellow teeth. His whole being seems to have taken on the hue of a chain-smoker's fingers. Owen's dad would have said he looked jaundiced. Would probably have given him some herbal remedy to fix it.

Here, now, Owen sees the truth of his former friend. Tony is more than ugly. He has a feral quality to him. His movements are those of a half-mad animal, a thing raised on violence and nourished on scraps of rotten meat.

Do it now, he thinks. Grab him. Smash your fist into his nasty little face. Make it make sense.

He feels the comforting pressure of the gun inside his

jacket. He's never fired one before. Hopes that he will not blink when he has to pull the trigger, that it doesn't kick the way the Albanian man warned him when he made the purchase in the little pink pub round the back of Hull Prison a year ago.

Do it...

OWEN SMILES. Waves.

Tony comes closer, unsure whether to stick out his hand. He settles on a smile and a gesture at the Heavens.

"Lovely day for it," he says.

"You alone?" asks Owen.

"Who the Hell else would be out on a day like today?"

Owen nods and feels the rain run down his face.

Then he looks up. Into him. Through him. Through Tony H. The man who killed her. Who killed them all. He feels that if he just stares hard enough, he'll see it playing out in the little man's eyes. See his confession. His fantasies. His memories of what he did.

Owen shivers in the cold.

"We gonna get under a tree or something?" Tony asks. "Got a few questions for you. Weird place to meet. I'd have chosen somewhere with fewer memories."

"I'll bet," Owen says, and the effort of speech weakens him. He is reluctant even to let go of a breath. He doesn't want the strength that has got him here to escape onto the breeze.

"You're not looking well," Tony adds. "You okay?"

Owen blinks raindrops from his eyes and tries to remember what he was supposed to say.

"You killed Ella Butterworth," he mutters, in a spray of mist. Then, more forcefully: "I know, Tone. I know what you've been doing."

"What?"

"How many more?"

"What are you talking about?"

"Your old number. It was in her phone. Messages about watching her. Liking what she was wearing. You killed her." Owen pauses. Grinds his teeth. "How many more?"

Tony's face, so practised in deception, twists into a mask of confusion. He looks baffled. Hurt.

"Was it because she wouldn't go near you? She looked at you and saw a dirty ugly bastard and decided not to let you near her?"

Owen feels his temper rise as he looks into the emotionless eyes of his fellow journalist. Unbidden, memories rise. He finds his mind filling with the photograph of the dead girl. Her father had given it to him in a hand wet with tears. Owen sees her smile. Sees the kindness in her eyes and the light upon her skin. She died in her wedding gown, stabbed forty-seven times through the stomach, chest and face with a weapon that has never been recovered. Five miles from here, the degenerate who found her body and took it home is standing trial for her murder. But while the man in the dock is guilty of much, he did not kill her. Nor did he kill the five other girls, all butchered by a man who took as much pleasure in writing about their deaths as he did in hacking them down.

"You were freelancing in every city where they died," says Owen, locking his teeth. "You couldn't resist it. I've seen the aliases you used for the by-lines. I've seen the addresses where the cheques were sent. It was you, you fuck. That night, the night she died ... you made me forget. You knew I'd drink the lot, you bastard. You knew I'd wake up next morning not knowing what my own bloody name was, let alone whether you slipped out in the night. She was beautiful, Tony. But you couldn't just look, could you. You had to have her. And when she said no you started hating her, like so many others. You stalked her. You sent her anonymous messages from a phone that only a few people know you own. And you hunted her down. You never thought I'd put the pieces together. But I know. That copper showed me her mobile phone history. He doesn't believe Cadbury killed her any more than I do. I recognised the number, you prick!"

Owen feels his hands becoming fists. Forces himself to breathe.

"She'd done nothing," he says, and pushes his long hair back from his face. It exposes the ugly red wound, held together with tape, that he suffered just hours ago on the floor of the custody suite at Queen's Gardens Police Station. He feels a sudden urge to lift up his shirt and show Tony the other bruises that he suffered at the hands and feet of the young detective constable who really wanted to show his boss what he could do.

Owen stares into Tony's eyes. Sees himself, staring back, and the swaying trees and the warring branches and the tumbling, tumbling rain.

"Owen, wait..."

"You dirty, dirty bastard."

"Easy now..."

"You didn't deserve to touch her. To breathe the same air. For you to be the last thing she saw..."

And Tony unleashes the killer within. Drops of red explode like dying stars in his eyes, as blood-vessels burst with the enormity of his fury.

He barrels towards Owen and takes him in the middle with a strength that he does not look as though he possesses. Tony's body is a pestilent, fragile thing; all tissue and twigs. But there is a venom inside him that makes him strong and he takes down the bigger, younger man in one angry jerk. The breath escapes from Owen's lungs in a rush. His hands fly up and the gun lands wetly on the sodden path as they thump onto the ground; Owen's head smacking back with a dizzying thud.

Tony is astride him, forearm beneath his chin, pushing down on his wind-pipe, staring into him.

Then deeper.

A more terrible aspect to his face than anything Owen's mind has ever conjured.

Spitting poison, spraying rage.

"You're right you soft prick! I didn't deserve to touch her. Didn't deserve to touch any of them. Not like you. Not like a handsome bastard who doesn't know what he's got. Not worth fucking trying because I can already see it in their eyes. That knowledge that they're better than me. They think it's a game. Winding me up. Getting me going. Slagging around in their short skirts with their tits out, begging the world to look at them. Well, I looked. I fell for it, time and again. And then I ended it. Became something more important than a fuck. Whatever happens, the most important thing anybody will remember about these pretty girls is the way they died. And every time their deaths are spoken of, they'll be talking about me. Nobody else can ever have that. Nobody!"

Spit froths from Tony's purplish, blubbery lips and lands among the raindrops on Owen's face as hands tighten around his throat and squeeze the breath from his body and the thoughts from his mind. Thunder roars in his skull.

His vision dwindles to a point, like an old TV being switched off; everything spiralling down into one tiny blob of colour.

Desperately, he reaches around on the forest floor, fingers scrabbling for a branch. For something solid.

Tony slams his spare hand down on his forehead.

Again.

Again.

Owen feels as though his own tongue is halfway down his throat, as though his eyes are going to explode. He tries to get an arm free but there's nothing to hit. Tony's all bony elbows and sharp fists, wet clothes and loose skin. It's like fighting a long-dead corpse.

There is a solid meaty thump, and then the pressure is gone; the figure on Owen's chest disappears in a blur and slithers onto the wet ground.

Owen is on his knees, retching, massaging his throat. Through blurred, watery eyes, he makes out Tony pulling himself to his feet. He's reaching inside his dirty, sodden coat.

Pulling out the murder weapon.

It's a kukri: a curved blade used by the Ghurkhas of the Nepalese Armed Forces. Pictures of it have been appearing in the Hull Mail for months. Tony wrote most of the articles.

Owen squints at the weapon. Sees Ella Butterworth's blood on the blade.

He hears a sound behind him.

The policeman is sprawled out like a toppled statue, trying

to find his feet on the sloping, slippery surface, a look of panic on his broad face...

McAvoy.

For a second, Tony seems unsure which direction to advance, whether to finish off the copper who pulled him from his prey, or gut his best friend before he can get his breath.

McAvoy finds his feet and hauls himself up, emerging from the puddles and the dirt and the leaves. He's big enough to snap Tony in two. Seems almost big enough to pull one of the oaks from the ground and smash it on the murderer's ratty head.

"Stop," he shouts.

He's holding the gun in a massive white fist. The barrel shakes and trembles. There is absolute terror in his eyes.

Owen looks at the young policeman, with his red hair and his cheap suit and the look of earnest willingness in his eyes. He doesn't belong here in the blood and filth where people like Tony wade.

As he looks at him, Owen knows, to his very bones, that it is not in McAvoy's nature to pull the trigger.

Tony laughs. Gives Owen a glance and a wink, as if they're still old pals in the press room making fun of the new boy. Then he runs at McAvoy.

He slashes down with the kukri. McAvoy raises his hands in a boxer's stance and the blade hits the metal of the gun. It falls from his hand. He steps back and loses his footing as Tony hacks at him. The blade digs into his collarbone like an axe into firewood. Tony has to yank it hard to get it free. McAvoy is on his back, a look of broken-hearted bewilderment upon his big, trusting face. Tony chops down again.

McAvoy jerks like a dying fish as the rainbow of thick blood arcs upwards and patters onto the earth.

Tony turns back to Owen, his face crimson, eyes wide and terrible.

He picks up the gun.

He points it at Owen's chest. Gives a shrug that could almost be apology. Pulls the trigger.

The bullet thuds into the tree trunk and Tony yells as he

totters off balance. McAvoy's shove in the back of the knees has cost him his shot.

Owen's eyes follow the gun as it pinwheels through the rain and bounces off a branch to nestle on a pillow of sycamore leaves. He takes half a dozen, desperate, frantic paces, and dives for it. He swivels and focuses, eyes on the man who has taken everything from him.

The last time Owen pulled a trigger he was a child and the weapon was a shotgun. He killed a wood pigeon and the guilt never left him.

He does not have the capacity to take a life. But he knows how to save one.

He pulls the trigger.

Tony's mouth opens as his eyes turn black and for a moment he has the look of a shark, crashing upwards through sea and spray to close his jaws around something fragile. Then his knees give way.

He collapses amid the mulch of the clearing, a dark stain spreading outwards from the ruination beneath his belly, as he clutches himself and hisses on the forest floor. Blood seeps through his fingers through the ragged, hanging wound between his legs.

Gasping for breath, Owen crawls to where McAvoy kneels, one hand pressed to the gash at his collar-bone. His face is a mess: more meat than skin.

"Is he dead?" McAvoy asks, and the effort seems to lighten his skin tone by several shades. He is the colour of dirty chalk.

"No," says Owen, his throat raw. "But he's going to need a needle and thread to fiddle with himself in prison."

"You didn't kill him?"

"No."

"Why?"

"Why didn't you?"

"I'm not a killer."

McAvoy's breathing begins to sound unnatural. He blinks, furiously, as the rain hits his staring eyes. Owen wonders what the big man can see, here in this place between life and death.

"Roisin," he says, and the word becomes a sob. "I wanted it to work ..."

"You'll be okay," says Owen, and wishes he meant it. "Where's your phone? Your radio?"

McAvoy says nothing, and Owen has to scrabble through his pockets. He finds the phone in the inside pocket of his jacket. Pulls it out with fingers dripping blood. He dials 999. Looks down at the dying policeman and wonders if Doug Roper will give a damn.

They sit in the rain, wind tearing at their skins, their wounds, listening to Tony's sobs and curses.

Owen holds up McAvoy's phone. The picture on the screen-saver is a beautiful, dark-haired girl with hooped earrings and too much lip-gloss. If he knew her name he would call her.

He presses his hand on the ugly trench of ruptured skin on McAvoy's front. Feels splintered bone. For a second he is troubled by a selfish, disloyal question: what will happen to him? Only McAvoy believed him. Only McAvoy promised to help clear his name if he helped catch a killer in return. But McAvoy is dying. And Doug Roper wants Owen in the ground.

As he feels McAvoy's big heart begin to flutter beneath his palm, Owen looks at McAvoy's phone. Something sparks in his mind. He knows Roper. How he operates. He knows he will be searched within moments of the blue lights appearing through the trees. Knows, too, that Roper will need to save face.

He lifts McAvoy's phone and punches in a number he knows by heart.

He slips the mobile back into the dying man's pocket.

The sound of sirens grows louder, even as the pulse under his hands fades away...

1

Different venue.

Different coroner.

Different world.

Were he pushed, Inmate HN 6781 would admit to finding the changes a little disquieting. He'd had a picture in his mind of what to expect. He used to know the old courtroom like the palm of his mind. Knew the girls by name. Ate biscuits with the old coroner in his warm, private office while talking over changes in the law. He'd been a nice chap. Avuncular, smartly dressed; friendly, even. Took the time to tell the local reporters when they should put a note in their diary. Had a nose for news, and always returned a favour.

Better times. A better life.

It hadn't previously occurred to Inmate HN 6781 that the world would have moved on in his absence. He had prepared himself to be recognised. Had steeled himself for a few pitying stares. He thought he might even have made one or two of the female officers blush. Imagined them greeting him like a much-missed friend and enquiring about his well-being; his where-abouts these past few years, too-late in noticing the cuff on his left wrist and the man in prison blues standing like a shadow a pace behind him.

In his last interview with his personal officer at HMP Bull

Sands, Inmate HN 6781 gave away an uncharacteristic confidence. He told her that he coped with his incarceration by imagining himself in a state of suspended animation. Sees himself as static. Imagines things remaining the same in his absence. He likes to imagine that the world is on hold, like a buffering internet connection, while he is away. His personal officer picked holes in the coping strategy. Had asked him how he could possibly feel that way when so much had already altered. His father had died during his imprisonment. His partner had left him. He had lost his home, been declared bankrupt and been brutally beaten a half dozen times since his sentencing. How could he even think of returning to a world unchanged? Inmate HN 6781 did not offer a reply.

"I preferred Essex House," he says, glumly, looking down at the scruffy wooden floor. He examines the mosaic of intermingled footprints left by the men and women who sit behind and around him, uncomfortable in blue, high-backed chairs, playing with their phones or staring at nothing as they wait for the coroner to come back and tell them they can leave.

"Sorry it's not up to your standards," says Mr Hills, seated to his left. "I did ask if they could hire a five-star hotel and bring a butler to wait you on you but they said it was too short notice."

"Sorry, sir."

"Aye."

Inmate HN 6781 keeps his eyes on the floor. The tall man to his left doesn't like being stared at too hard. Inmate HN 6781 uses only his peripheral vision to check what the man he is handcuffed to is occupying himself with. Notices that he is scrolling through Facebook on his phone and liking posts that suggest foreigners are, broadly speaking, the problem. He has taken off his raincoat and hung it on the back of his chair, where it is dripping melted snow onto the feet of the woman behind him. She chose to wear Ugg boots this morning despite three inches of slush. It now looks as though she has her feet stuffed into two dead meerkats, and the court is filling with a smell of damp socks and wet dog.

He looks ahead of him, at the public gallery. The woman with the black hair is Will's mum. She's plump and wears a lot of purple. She's in her late forties but could be twenty years older. She keeps dabbing her nose with a balled-up tissue, exposing the lacy cuffs of a cheap velvet jacket. She's got silver rings on each finger and a stud in her nose. There's a twisted metal pendant on a cord around her neck and a Green Man tattoo pokes out the top of her blouse, winking lopsidedly from her left breast. She smells of incense and cats.

Prisoner HN 6781 looks away. He doesn't want to catch her eye. Doesn't want to tell his lies to somebody who knows a different truth.

"I don't think much of this coroner," he says to Mr Hills, trying again to make conversation. "Last bloke was really friendly. Properly put people at their ease, y'know."

Mr Hills grunts. He's been a prison officer for 14 years. He's been handcuffed to hundreds of inmates. He long ago stopped giving a damn who his charges were before they became his responsibility and his problem. The man he's looking after today used to be a journalist in this part of the world. Kept chattering about it on the drive up. He seemed almost excited as they crossed the Humber Bridge and were enveloped in a grey swirl of snow-filled cloud.

Inmate HN 6781 decides to be quiet. Mr Hills is a decent enough officer. He's professional and courteous, if not exactly brimming over with compassion. He's treated him decently enough today. Even walked shoulder to shoulder, so the chain that held them together wouldn't be immediately visible.

"You think he'll be long?" asks Mr Hills, looking at his phone.

Prisoner HN 6781 enjoys being asked for his expert opinion. He makes a meal of his answer, giving it full and detailed consideration.

"Another few minutes," he says. "Court closes for lunch at 12.30. The coroner's got two hearings this afternoon. If he comes back from his deliberations at 12-ish then that gives him time to deliver his decision and shut up shop. Have himself a long lunch."

Mr Hills gives a begrudging grunt of thanks. Inmate HN 6781 enjoys it, though he wishes his answer had been different.

He would have liked the hearing to go on all week. As it is, the whole thing was dealt with in under an hour. The statements were read out without cross-examination. His own witness report was read by a short, round-faced officer of the court. It hadn't sounded any more truthful in her voice than it had in his own.

He leans forward. He's seated at an angle to the press bench and can't see what the young reporter is typing on his laptop because his back and shoulders are in the way. Inmate HN 6781 would love to read the words, if only to revel in superiority. He has no doubt he will find spelling and grammatical errors, and he is sure that it will start with three relatively interesting paragraphs, before tailing off into legalese and bullshit.

Inmate HN 6781 used to be called Owen Swainson. He used to be a journalist in this city. Used to sit at the press bench and write about people with more interesting lives than his own. Then he helped catch a serial killer and went to prison for his trouble. He has not been back to Hull since the judge at the Crown Court building, less than 50 yards from where he now sits, told him he was going to prison for a very long time.

As he sits inside the Guildhall and waits for the coroner to come and deliver a verdict that was a foregone conclusion even before the hearing began, Owen wonders if the judge would recognise him. His long dark hair is now a dirty grey and there is little meat on his bones. His skin has the pale, greenish tinge of an old alabaster headstone and his T-shirt and prison-issue jeans hide scars, bruises and bones that are broken as often as they are not. He has suffered in prison.

Owen senses movement and looks up to find that the journalist has left his seat. The article he was writing is still on the screen. Owen squints to make it out and smiles as he notices that the journalist has left space at the bottom for the closing quotes and verdict. The top half of the story will clearly not be affected by whatever it is the coroner says when he returns from his deliberations.

. . .

A CONVICTED drug dealer was horrifically killed when he became caught in a drilling machine while on day-release at a farm in East Yorkshire, a court heard.

William Blaylock, 23, suffered multiple injuries when he became entangled with the auger while working at Shepton Farm, near Gilberdyke, in June this year.

Mr Blaylock, originally from Ipswich, was a prisoner at Bull Sands Open Prison near Mablethorpe, where he was serving a 16-month sentence for possession of a controlled drug with intent to supply.

The Category-D prisoner had recently become eligible to apply for work as part of a successful rehabilitation programme run by the prison. Having spent time on the prison's own farm and shown an interest in agriculture, he was given a temporary position at the farm belonging to Mr Ronald Erskine.

On the day of the incident, Mr Blaylock was working alone in an outbuilding when it appears his clothing became entangled with the large, petrol-powered auger stored there. The drill has a diameter of 8" and spins at 150rpm. He was dragged into the machine and suffered catastrophic wounds to his sternum.

The alarm was raised by other workers at the farm – among them a fellow inmate.

Owen Swainson, 37, told the court in a statement: "I heard the scream and ran as quickly as I could but by the time I got to the building there was nothing I could do. There was a huge amount of blood and it was clear he was beyond help. I held his hand until help arrived but I don't think he knew I was there. It was a terrible, terrible accident."

Mr Swainson, a former journalist, was previously a Hull resident and was sentenced for a vicious assault on a local woman which came to light during the hunt for the killer of Ella Butterworth.

At yesterday's hearing at Hull Coroner's Court, a solicitor for HMP Bull Sands explained that Mr Blaylock had been a model prisoner and had been hoping to work on a farm full-time after his release.

A report carried out by the Health and Safety Executive found that while the auger should not have been accessible to untrained staff, there were no indications Mr Erskine was at fault. A solicitor for Mr Erskine said that he had offered work to many serving and former prisoners and felt terrible about what had occurred.

HULL CORONER, DONALD HAYNES, SAID: "*."
Verdict: "*" (probably guilty).

OWEN KEEPS HIS FACE EXPRESSIONLESS. He has grown good at that over the last four years. He will not let himself smile unless there is a good reason for him to be seen doing so. Will not allow temper or frustration to alter his countenance. He has become a decent actor, over the years. When he begs them to stop hurting him it's because he knows that such utterances are what they seek. When he cries on his bunk, hugging his knees, it's because he knows he is being watched. Today, on the drive from HMP Bull Sands, he exuded excitable giddiness for the benefit of the bus driver and Mr Hills. He'd known that his demeanour would get back to those who pull his strings. If he appeared introspective, they might have worried that he was thinking about giving vent to his conscience and baring his soul about what really happened that day on the farm. Instead, he chose to appear schoolboy-like. To go on and on about who he used to be. He doesn't want them knowing what he truly feels about anything. Needs to keep them all guessing, right up until the end.

"All stand."

Own rises, bringing Mr Hills to his feet and feeling the metal of the cuff pull on his wrist. The coroner marches, straight-backed, to his chair and gives a curt nod before sitting down. The assembled witnesses, officers and lawyers make themselves comfortable and the young hack scurries to his seat.

Owen doesn't listen to the verdict. The solicitors at the table nearest the front represent the prison service, the Health and Safety Executive and Mr Erskine, the owner of the farm where Will died. They will all be happy with a verdict of accidental death.

Owen stares at the journalist's back. Wishes he could grab the laptop and write the truth. Wonders if anybody would even believe him.

Several times since his incarceration, Owen has started writing a book. Each time he has seen it destroyed.

Inmate HN 6781 can control the way people perceive him. He can appear broken and beaten. Can seem fool, failure and victim. But Inmate HN 6781 is a performance. Owen Swainson is not. Owen Swainson is a man so full of hate and rage that sometimes he thinks it will burst through his skin and consume him. His every thought is of retribution. He wants to thrust his hands into his tormentor's chest and pull apart the bones of his ribcage. He never thought he would hate anybody more than he hated Tony Halthwaite. But then Aector McAvoy betrayed him. As he sits and listens to the coroner regurgitate lies, Owen remembers that day on the farm; the day they skewered Will to the floor and tore through his guts with a drill the width of a dustbin-lid.

2

Detective Sergeant Aector McAvoy pulls his hat down and his collar up as he watches the snow fall half-heartedly from a grubby sky. A sharp wind is blowing in off the river, bringing with it a smell of petrol, fish-meal and tarmac. It makes gooseflesh rise beneath his shirt, jumper and waterproofed coat. He gives a theatrical shiver, attempting to blend in with the other pedestrians fitfully trembling themselves insensible at this dismal bus-stop on Hull's Alfred Gelder Street. McAvoy doesn't profess to be much of an actor but he believes his shiver to be quite convincing.

"Stop shaking so much," comes the voice in his ear. "You look like a dog shaking itself dry."

McAvoy grew up in the Highlands of Scotland, in a tumble-down croft built halfway up a mountain. For half the year its old stones were battered with hail, wind and snow. The hardships made him pretty much immune to the cold. So too did his size. He's a huge man, the sort of person that children stare at in the street. With his greying red hair and his angry scars, he has the air of a warrior about him. He's not an obvious choice for surveillance work.

"Still nothing. Still inside," says McAvoy, softly, into his lapel. "Still a horrible day."

"Stamp your feet," comes the voice. "But not too roughly – you'll start an avalanche."

McAvoy hides his smile. His boss, Superintendent Trish Pharaoh, is back in the warmth of the control room, watching the operation on CCTV. When the suspect emerges from the bank across the road, McAvoy will follow him on foot until he is told to hand off to one of the other officers dotted around the Old Town. He hasn't seen anybody he recognises yet. He only knows the face of the suspect because it was on the whiteboard at this morning's briefing. Pharaoh's Serious and Organised Unit has been drafted in to help the Major Incident Team from West Mercia Constabulary. They have evidence that the middle-aged, balding man busily discussing his borrowing requirements with a blonde cashier is responsible for three murders on their patch. McAvoy doesn't know the background of the case well enough to pass judgement. He just knows it's his job to keep an eye on him, and not let the bugger disappear.

"I'm drinking a hot chocolate," comes the voice in his ear. "It's warm and creamy, with extra marshmallows."

"You're cruel," says McAvoy, slightly louder than he intended. The short, grey-haired woman to his right looks at him curiously, then turns away. She hasn't reached a ripe old age by questioning big, scarred nutters on their conversations with invisible people.

"It's got a Flake in it."

"I can't hear you."

McAvoy pulls his hat down, giving him a chance to shield his smile with his hand. He looks up at the sky, past the roofs of the old buildings that were built as merchant houses and municipal centres and are now home to solicitors, estate agents and copy-shops. The snow isn't particularly thick. This morning, over breakfast, McAvoy told his six-year-old son that the sky was so grim it made the windows look dirty. Fin paused to give the matter some thought, before opining that it seemed as if somebody was grating a giant snowman over East Yorkshire. Fin's teachers occasionally worry about his imagination. McAvoy revels in it.

To his right, a single-decker bus is cruising through the grey slush that has been heaped into matching peaks by endless tyres.

"Bus approaching. View Obscured. Switch to Team B."

"Understood."

McAvoy steps back. Gives the old ladies at the bus stop a kindly smile and indicates they should go first. He looks to his left. Half a dozen black cabs stand at the taxi rank; their windows steamed up as their drivers read newspapers and drink tea. Taxis are a luxury here. The ladies waiting for the bus to the Bransholme estate could feed themselves for a week on the cost of getting a cab home. They use their bus passes and endure their cold. They're of a generation that remembers when Hull mattered. When kids left school at fourteen and took a job on a trawler, sailing to distant waters to do battle with the elements in exchange for a decent wage. But when the industry died, so did Hull's fortunes. For all of the money that has been pumped into the city, it remains on its arse. The schools are at the foot of the league tables and crime and unemployment are high. Despite its beautiful architecture and good-natured people, it's a hard city. It has suffered. McAvoy feels at home here. He's suffered too.

"Team B not in place. Vision blocked. McAvoy, change position."

McAvoy turns away from the bus shelter. He fumbles in his pocket for his mobile phone and pretends to be making a call as he walks, using the reflection in the shop windows to his right to check that the suspect is still at the cashier's desk across the street. There is a moment's panic as he notices that he is no longer at the head of the queue. He turns and looks directly at the bank, staring hard through the darkened glass. The door swings open and Michael Lenneville emerges, walking quickly past the entrance to Hull Council's customer service centre. He pauses at a window covered with posters offering help and advice. McAvoy isn't sure if the staff inside are trained for this particular challenge.

McAvoy considers the suspect. He's 5ft 8" and thirty-seven years old. Overweight. He's turning around, furtively. He breaks

stride when he notices the giant across the road, staring at him
too hard.

McAvoy looks away staring at his mobile phone.

"I think he's spotted me. Pulling back."

"Shit, Team B are blocked in. There's a bloody van parked
on the slipway. Who've we got on foot?"

The radio crackles and McAvoy hears the voice of Ben
Neilsen. "Poised at Guildhall, Guv. Andy's in Queen's Gardens.
West Mercia still in position – two officers by the suspect's car."

Across the road, Lenneville starts to walk.

"McAvoy, stand by."

Lenneville throws a look over his shoulder. Stares again at
McAvoy. Starts to run.

Trish Pharaoh swears.

"Hector, get after him!"

"Christ!"

McAvoy steps into the road just as a security van turns left out
of Parliament Street. The driver slams on his breaks and the slush
thrown up by the tyres soaks McAvoy to the waist as he begins
running down Parliament Street. To his left is the rear of the
Guildhall; all old, rectangular stone and weather-beaten wooden
doors. He can hear Trish barking orders in his ear, telling Ben
Neilsen that she doesn't give a damn if the arrest strategy hasn't
been approved. She tells him to put himself between Lenneville
and freedom and to punch whoever he needs to.

Ahead, Lenneville is throwing panicky glances over his
shoulder as he puff and pants his way towards the crossroads.
In the distance is Hull Crown Court; to his right two pubs and a
pool hall. The few shoppers who have ventured out on this grey
day stop to watch the big man chase the fat man through the
snow.

"Sarge, I see him!"

Lenneville disappears as he darts left towards the front of
the Guildhall. McAvoy plunges forward and follows in the foot-
steps of the man he is starting to hate for making him run.

"Fuck, watch it!"

McAvoy careers into a figure in blue, sending it pinwheeling away in a flash of arms, legs and curses. The figure crashes into another and they tumble to the ground with a damp, painful splat. McAvoy's head has struck a skull and he sees stars for a moment, but the shouting of his name clears his head. He looks up to find DC Ben Neilsen sitting on Michael Lenneville, one hand twisted up his back and his face pushed into the snow. McAvoy lets out a sigh and looks down at the two people who were unfortunate enough to get in his way.

His face changes as he takes in the men before him. They are handcuffed together. One wears a blue prison uniform beneath a dirty raincoat. He's rubbing his forehead with his free hand and there is blood coming from his nose. The second man is kneeling, almost as if in prayer. His face is thinner and the darkness beneath his eyes looks as though it was put there with a coal-smudged thumb.

But there is no mistaking the man who once saved his life.

The man looks up and recognition flashes in his eyes. A look of utter hatred disturbs the features of his face, like a rock thrown in a pond. And then he is being yanked to his feet by the prison officer.

"Sarge, I could use a hand!"

McAvoy feels as though his guts are full of snow. His mind fills with pictures he has not allowed himself to study in four years. He has a sudden memory of dead leaves and sideways rain and hands trying to stuff the blood back into his body as he dribbled onto nothing on the cold, hard ground.

"Owen..."

"The fuck you playing at, ya big bastard?" snarls the prison officer, pushing himself so close to McAvoy that his angry words arrive in a hiss of spray.

"Sarge..."

"I'm sorry," begins McAvoy, though he isn't sure who he's apologising too.

In his ear: "Hector, have you fucking got him or what?"

"You could have broken my bloody skull!"

"Guv, I'm not sure..."

"Hector, what the hell is going on?"

"Sarge!"

"If I wasn't in uniform I'd smash your face in, you ginger prick!"

"Sarge?"

McAvoy turns and sees that Lenneville is struggling in Ben's grasp. Through the tangle of onlookers he sees Andy Daniells, even more portly than the suspect, waddling quickly through the snow.

"I'm a policeman," says McAvoy, distractedly, trying to get the prison officer to stop shouting at him.

In his ear: "I know you bloody are. But could you be a good policeman rather than a shit one and tell me what the fuck's happening. I've got you on CCTV. Who's the bloke with the cuffs? Hector!"

McAvoy feels eyes upon him; eyes that seem to stare up at him from a dark, black place far beneath his feet.

"Owen," says McAvoy, and the name feels alien on his tongue. "Why? What's happening?"

"Hector!"

"Sarge!"

McAvoy turns away from the cold eyes and sees his colleagues struggling with their prisoner. He can hear sirens and raised voices among the smokers and motorists who have stopped their days to gawp.

McAvoy runs towards the struggling figures and places a hand on the suspect's back. Leans in with just enough pressure to let him know that, if he should choose, he could leave him looking like a fossil.

Lenneville stops moving.

McAvoy turns back to where he left the two men.

Sees only empty air, and melting snow.

3

Lights flashing, sirens blaring, ambulance and police van pulling up as close to the Guildhall as the driver can manage: its crew leaping out in green overalls, dragging equipment, barking instructions, questions, cursing the snow...

Police cars. Pharaoh's little convertible, abandoned at the centre of Hull's busiest T-junction, wedged in among the bigger vehicles like a comma between words.

Press. Satellite dishes on roofs. Journalists tucking shirts into their trousers and pulling Wellingtons from the trunks of cars.

"Could have been worse," says Pharaoh, sipping coffee from a mug that declares her the World's Best Dad.

She and McAvoy are staring out of the window of one of the more attractive function rooms on the ground floor of the Guildhall. McAvoy thinks he may have been at a wedding here.

McAvoy raises his own mug to his lips. It has a picture of a squirrel on it. He doesn't know where the uniformed officer rustled up the hot drinks, but he's grateful. He's soaked to the bone.

"West Mercia are happy enough," continues Pharaoh, giving him a nudge that suggests he cheer up.

"It didn't go quite according to plan," mutters McAvoy,

turning away from the chaos beyond the leaded glass and giving a sigh that blows Pharaoh's dark hair back from her face and makes her dangly earrings rattle.

"They were hoping he would lead them to whoever he'd been planning on taking next. They wanted to catch him in the act so there would be no loopholes come the court case. But it doesn't matter now. He was already confessing when they led him away."

McAvoy sucks his lower lip. "He was definitely guilty then."

Pharaoh gives a little grin and exposes the shiny tooth in her top set. It's whiter than the others. She's still waiting for a permanent replacement for the incisor that was kicked out by a drug dealer on Flamborough Head. The Police Federation's insurers are playing silly beggars over who should foot the bill since she wasn't officially on duty when she sustained the injury.

"You don't seem thrilled," says Pharaoh, slapping him on the chest with the back of her hand. "I saw what happened on the monitors. Don't be embarrassed, you didn't even fall over. I couldn't have run five yards in that slush."

McAvoy shakes his head.

"Is it Roisin?" asks Pharaoh, cocking her head, like a bird that has heard a worm beneath the ground. "Everything's okay, yeah? She's pleased to be home? You're still love's young dream?"

McAvoy gives a tired laugh. The look on Pharaoh's face when she mentions his wife is the same one that Roisin wears when she mentions his boss.

"The prisoner," says McAvoy, at last. "The one I knocked over. I knew him. Know him. However you want to put it."

Pharaoh drains her drink and puts the mug down on an ugly wooden table, which she perches herself upon. She crosses her arms and gives him her full attention, tucking her sunglasses into her cleavage and staring at him with eyes that he can never allow himself to look into for long.

"You sent him down?" she asks.

McAvoy licks his teeth and feels momentarily angry. Tells himself to breathe. Closes his eyes.

"You know when I got hurt..."

"Which time?" asks Pharaoh, smiling.

"The first time, I suppose you'd call it. Humber Bridge."

Pharaoh's smile fades. She knows. Everybody knows. "When you caught Tony Halthwaite," she says.

McAvoy takes two steps to his left and leans against one of the columns.

"What do you remember?" he asks, quietly.

Pharaoh gives his arm a squeeze. "I remember a lot, Hector. Remember meeting a big lump of a copper who was scared of his own shadow. Remember a body in a bush and a Murder squad so corrupt it had started oozing out the door. I remember Roper, and how much I'd have enjoyed taking him down." She shakes her head, blue eyes catching the light. "You're getting me nostalgic."

McAvoy licks dry lips. Starts to talk.

"Ella Butterworth," he says, and in his soft Scottish accent, her name sounds strangely lyrical. "We had a chap for it. Shane Cadbury. Wasn't very bright. Don't know if there's a diagnosis for it but he wasn't somebody you'd want one of your daughters meeting for a drink. Ella's body was found at his flat. She was wearing her wedding dress. She'd been stabbed so many times that when they moved the body, the pathologist said it was like picking up a spider-web. I was first on the scene. I drove myself half mad after that. Couldn't get the smell of her out of my nose."

"Christ," breathes Pharaoh. "Go on."

"Doug Roper was leading the investigation..."

"...prick," says Pharaoh, automatically.

"...and it was his idea to search all the houses in the area near where she was last seen. She'd been trying on her dress, you see. Some red wine got spilled. She ran to her mum's house, two streets away. Never got there. Missing for three weeks. Roper leaned on everybody he could and got nowhere. The search was an act of desperation. But somehow it worked. Like I said, we found her."

Pharaoh holds up her hand and shakes her head. "*You*

found her, Hector. Everybody knows it was you, and what you saw."

McAvoy looks away. Stops himself remembering.

"Roper charged Cadbury with her murder in no time. But Cadbury said something to me that wouldn't go away. He said he'd found her, laid out and gift-wrapped. He never elaborated on it. Never got much of a chance to. He had convictions for sex offences and he abused her body enough to leave plenty of DNA."

"But you had doubts?"

"I just wanted to be sure," says McAvoy, and shivers as he remembers what it was to be the new boy on the team of Humberside Police's brightest star. Doug Roper was handsome, charming and utterly merciless in his pursuit of convictions. His clean-up rate was the envy of every CID team in the UK, and while some questioned his methods, he was ruthlessly efficient. He hadn't wanted McAvoy on his close-knit team, but an opening came up and Roper was short-handed. He accepted the earnest sergeant with bad grace and treated him as little more than a gopher. McAvoy felt a duty to Ella. He endured the jibes and the pointless assignments. Put up with it all to help catch a killer.

"I probably shouldn't have done it but I'd put together this kind of computerised Venn diagram system," he says, lost in memory. "It was a basic prototype but it was designed to pick out similarities between cases and extrapolate a list of connected crimes, solved or unsolved. I'd linked it to all the existing databases. There was a pattern to Ella's wounds. They were inflicted with something that might have been a kukri – the knife used by Gurkhas. And there were several cases from up and down the country where such a weapon had been used. I did some digging and read some articles about the victims. In two separate locations, I recognised the by-line of a reporter. I thought they might know more than they printed so I requested their details. It turned out the by-line was a pseudonym of the same freelance who was working for the Hull Mail and covering the Ella Butterworth case. Tony Halthwaite."

"Good police work," says Pharaoh. "Roper should have done it."

"I didn't know it but a local reporter was putting the same pieces together. His name was Owen Swainson. Trouble was, he approached Roper with his findings. Roper had him arrested. He got some girl to say Swainson'd stuck a gun in her face and sexually assaulted her. Roper had one of his junior officers put a beating on him. I broke it up."

Pharaoh gives a quick smile. "I bet you did."

"After he was bailed, we compared notes. I didn't know what the hell to do. Roper was everything I hated in a police officer. He didn't give a damn about the truth, he just wanted the result. Thing is, Owen was Tony's alibi. Tony's car was in the area when Ella disappeared, but he said that it was taken for a joyride while he was drinking with Owen. Owen was too drunk to remember differently."

"You decided to take Tony down yourself," says Pharaoh. McAvoy knows she's wanted this conversation ever since she first took him under her wing. She seems like she wants to put her hand on his arm.

"I was still deciding what to do when Owen lost his mind. He arranged to meet Tony at the country park. It was a place they used to go and drink and put the world to rights of an evening. It all went wrong. I got hurt."

Pharaoh nods.

"While I was in hospital, Owen was charged and put on trial. It was all rushed through. He was advised to plead guilty to possessing an offensive weapon. That was true – he did own a gun. He'd bought it at the docks while doing an article on how easy it is to get a gun into the country. I don't know who Roper leaned on, but by the time I was fit to do anything other than bleed, Owen had been given nine years and sent to Wayland Prison. Roper quit before it came out that he nearly sent an innocent man to prison. Tony Halthwaite was declared mentally unfit and has been in Rampton ever since."

"And you?"

McAvoy gives a snort of contempt. "Doing better than Owen."

"You feel guilty?" asks Pharaoh, as kindly as she can.

"Every moment of every day."

"And that's who you bumped into today?"

McAvoy nods. "What was he doing here?"

Pharaoh manoeuvres her head until she is in his eyeline. Then she gives him her best smile. "I can tell you if you want."

McAvoy waits for his boss and friend to explain herself.

"I checked him out as soon as I saw a bloke in cuffs on the monitor. I'm a Detective Superintendent. I think things like that are important."

McAvoy is unsure whether to smile or scowl.

"It was only a couple of phonecalls," she says, shrugging. "And I've been waiting for you to tell me about that night for bloody years."

McAvoy gives in to a smile. It fades as he finds himself wondering what he is about to learn.

"He's not in Wayland any more," says Pharaoh, pulling her notebook from the recesses of her large, fake designer handbag and peering at it. "He's much closer to home. HMP Bull Sands. Category D, open prison. The sort that the Daily Mail calls a holiday camp, as if that makes it any less vile. Been there eight months. He was here giving evidence at an inquest into the death of a prisoner out on day release at a farm out towards Howden. He had to be here in case the solicitor acting for the farmer wanted to cross-examine him. Turned out he didn't. It was all pretty open and shut. Accidental death and nobody's fault. Owen will be halfway back down to Mablethorpe by now."

McAvoy realises he is standing too still. He has his hand across his mouth, one finger touching his nose and the others curved around his chin. He is staring at Pharaoh too intently. She catches his eye as she glances up from her notes and they both look down again. McAvoy colours and Pharaoh starts patting pockets for her cigarettes.

"Who died?" asks McAvoy, pointing at the left-hand side of Pharaoh's coat to remind her where she keeps her smokes.

"William Blaylock," says Pharaoh, pulling out the packet and holding one of the cigarettes beneath her nose to inhale it.

"Swainson's cell-mate, according to what I could get. Accident with farm machinery. Bloody great drill, right through the chest."

"The chest?" asks McAvoy, keeping a careful eye on his boss to make sure she doesn't light the cigarette indoors. "How's that an accident? What kind of drill?"

"Petrol-powered auger," reads Pharaoh. "Sounds like it would sting a bit. He was a dealer but low-rung."

"Poor lad."

"Aye."

McAvoy looks past her at the darkened windows. Realises that the lights of the ambulance are still flashing and that he has been bathed in blue light.

"Just noticed that, have you?" asks Pharaoh. "You look like a cross between a Jelly Baby and an Avatar. Very fetching."

McAvoy knows she is trying to shunt the great locomotive of his mind away from dwelling on his encounter with Owen. Roisin apart, she knows him better than anybody. Sometimes she seems to know him better than he does himself.

"I should have visited him," he says.

"Nobody could blame you for avoiding it," says Pharaoh. "You nearly died."

"I would have died if he hadn't saved me."

"The way I read it, he would have died if you hadn't saved him."

"But he's in prison for lies," says McAvoy, suddenly angry. "Roper set the whole thing up."

Pharaoh looks sceptical. "He was a prick, Hector, and he cut corners, but he wouldn't have had the power to send somebody to prison for nothing. And like you say, there was the gun crime. Sometimes shit happens to people. He'll probably write a book about it when he gets out and make a fortune. You've done him a favour. Give yourself a break."

McAvoy would usually smile in thanks but there is a tightness in his chest and he feels wet across his back. He realises how many walls he has built around the memory of that night in the woods. He has faced death more often than any person should but he has never come closer to losing everything than when he lay bleeding on that forest floor Suddenly, McAvoy has a strong vision of Owen cradling his young cellmate. Imagines tears in his eyes as the young man in his arms puddles into claret and flesh upon the floor of a dirty barn.

"Did you get a chance to ask about the post mortem?" asks McAvoy, quietly. "Any suggestion of other injuries? I mean, I don't want to cause him any more problems. Just turning up, like…"

Pharaoh holds the cigarette to her nose again and breathes in. She looks like she would be willing to bite off at least one limb to be allowed to light it indoors.

"It's Lincolnshire's patch," she warns. "Inquest is done. Nothing to do with us."

McAvoy looks affronted. "I didn't say anything!"

"Shush," she says, smiling. "I was going to suggest it anyway. Sounds like you've been waiting for an opportunity."

McAvoy feels an overwhelming desire to start the day over again. Wishes he had never seen the face from his past. But now he has, he knows that he cannot close down the memories that are suddenly seeping into every corner of his mind, flooding cracks and crevices like red wine running over marble.

"Saved the best for last," says Pharaoh, sweetly. "Blaylock and Swainson shared a wing with Mitchell Spear."

"Spear?"

"One of the faces who ran Francis Nock's operation in Newcastle. Moved to Bull Sands around the same time as Blaylock. Spear walked out about a fortnight before the kid died and hasn't come back since. I'm sure with a bit of creative thinking you could talk to Owen in connection with some alleged sighting. Speak to a few others too. It's a decent enough cover. Make it up to Owen, buy him a Kit-Kat, get yourself home for supper."

McAvoy chews on his lip. When they first met he would have thought that cutting any corners with the truth was diabolical. He did things entirely as the guidelines said they should be done and kept his personal feelings buried beneath layers of textbooks and bureaucracy. He would never have considered going onto another police service's patch and trying to make amends to a convicted prisoner by raking over a case that has already been solved.

Pharaoh looks at him softly. "Is it that you want to apologise? Or is it that you want to put your side of the story?"

McAvoy forces himself to meet her gaze.

"I just think that we have things to say to each other. Things I should have said. I was always too scared to even write to him. He looked awful, boss. Real pale and bruised. I did that to him. If this friend has died and there's more to it, maybe I could help put things right."

Pharaoh shakes her head, as if marvelling at the simplicity of his thinking.

"He might tell you to fuck off. Most people would, considering."

"I just want to help."

"They'll put that on your tombstone."

"I'm not being buried. I want to be scattered."

"I promise that when the time comes, you'll be scattered somewhere pretty – they just won't burn you first."

Pharaoh stands up and squeezes his arm. "Talk it through with Roisin. She might have something to say about you raking up the past. You've been through a lot. All I'm saying is, be careful. And if you want to go and talk to him, I've got your back."

McAvoy watches as she puts her sunglasses back on and pulls her biker jacket tight across her chest.

"Do you think I did wrong?" he asks her, staring at the wall.

"If you did, it's understandable," she says. "Forgivable, at least."

"No," says McAvoy, and then repeats it more firmly. "No, it's not."

4

The dead man lies beneath the scratchy woollen
blanket. Feels his own dead breath settle on his face.
He listens. The men who are trying to open the door
to his resting place are cursing. Blaming one another for their
inability to get inside this small, tumbledown shed on the allot-
ments at the back of the football ground.

The man on the bed doesn't stir. He has grown used to
biding his time.

Even though the men outside are making enough noise to
wake the dead, Raymond Mahon sees no sense in rushing his
resurrection.

Death suits Mahon. He has long looked as though his face
is half decomposed. Though he is a tall and well-muscled specimen, it is unquestionably his face that holds the attention.
Despite the many plastic surgeries, it is still a thing of horror. It
looks as though his face has been stitched together from ragged
flaps of other people's skin. He is a patchwork of lurid pinks
and leathery browns, stretched tight across the skull and
stapled to the jawbone. There is still a hole in his left cheek and
were it not for the scarf he wears across his face, his teeth and
tongue would be visible as he speaks. It is impossible to tell the
colour of his eyes. Large sunglasses perch on his nose, touching
the brim of his flat cap. With his leather jacket, black trousers

and military boots, he seems to be assembled entirely from clothing. He could pass for the Invisible Man.

Were he asked for his thoughts on his recent demise, he would probably say that not many people ever knew he was alive, and of those who did, most are dead themselves. As a young man he gave himself over, body and soul, to the criminal who would control the North East of England for the next fifty years. That man was Francis Nock. It was Mahon's honour and privilege to enforce Mr Nock's will. Mahon killed Mr Nock's enemies. Mahon kept Mr Nock safe. Mahon served countless years in prison and in hiding because in doing so, he spared Mr Nock from incarceration. Mahon was shot in the head and had his face eaten by pigs because Mr Nock made a mistake. And Mahon cared for the old man in his final months, feeding him his pills and changing his bed sheets and keeping his legend alive, even as other criminal outfits circled his territory like hyenas sensing a wounded animal. Last year Mr Nock died. So did Mahon. He plunged over a clifftop with one of Mr Nock's enemies in his hand and disappeared beneath the black water that pounded the rocks off Flamborough Head.

Mahon survived the fall. The man in Mahon's grip took most of the impact, cushioning his body as they slammed into the hard, barnacled stone. Waves pulled Mahon under. Held him down. He was aware only of a cold, crushing sadness, the vicious emptiness of his grief. He tried to give himself up to the sea. Instead, he was pitched onto shingle and sand. For an hour or more he lay on his back, watching storm clouds disperse and reform on the black sky, twisting and dissipating, like smoke around charred wood. Then he realised he was alive. Alive, and dead to all who knew him.

It hurt to stand but it hurt to lay still. Hurt to walk, but he walked anyway. He felt Mr Nock's absence the way a dog yearns for its master. He felt no freedom at being free of the man who held his leash for so many years. Were Mr Nock in the ground, Mahon would have lain down beside his headstone and put a bullet into his own brain. He saw no reason for his continued existence. He stole a car in the pretty village that looked down on the cove where his body washed ashore. Started driving with no real sense of direction, instinctively heading north. He passed police cars on the way, a strobe-light of blue illumination screeching past him towards the chaos he had left behind. In that moment, Mahon wondered if he was spared because Mr Nock still needed him to perform a service. He began to wonder if perhaps he could find purpose in revenge. A passage of Shakespeare came back to him. Something about grief softening the heart. "Think on revenge and cease to weep".

Mahon decided to fix himself.

To get well.

And then to kill every last fucker who helped stop Mr Nock's heart.

He finds himself thinking warmly about what is to come. Throughout his long life, Mahon despatched death dispassionately. He understands the enormity of such a thing: to snatch a person's entirety; to deny them all they will ever be. He killed pragmatically, without joy. That has changed these past months. The men he kills now, he kills for comfort. He kills them because he fucking well wants to.

The object of Mahon's wrath is a criminal outfit known to the police as the Headhunters. They started out down the coast in Hull and quickly branched out. Established crime outfits up and down the country were suddenly hit with demands for a share of their profits and territory. The crime bosses didn't know how to fight back. The new organisation was a shadow. It operated through anonymous phonecalls and quiet, faceless threats. The Headhunters were masters at finding young, ambitious and talented men within established crime families, and offering them the world. Nine times out of ten, ambition would win out. They would cut the head off their own outfit and assume control, kicking up a standard protection fee to the organisation that spotted their potential and quietly greased their wheels. Mr Nock held out against them and died for his troubles. In the months since, the territory he controlled for so long passed into the hands of the Flemyng brothers. They pay their tributes to the Headhunters and have the freedom to swagger around Newcastle as if they own the damn place. To Mahon they are an effrontery. They act the way they think they ought to having been raised on gangster films and The Wire. To Mahon, the North East is a graveyard; a monument to Mr Nock. And every footstep they take disturbs his rest.

Mahon is no longer as physically able as he used to be. Even before he tumbled from the cliffs, he was beginning to feel his age. Now he walks with a limp and his left arm is next to useless. He has a permanent ringing in his ears and when he wakes, the rattly wheeze that emerges from his chest puts him in mind of the ragged breaths of the dying. Mahon doesn't know how long he has. But he knows he will kill as many Headhunters as he can before the end.

"That's it! Kick it. Now!"

The wooden door of the shed refuses to yield under the pressure of the men's repeated kicks. When he chose this building as a place of execution, Mahon switched the hinges on the door jamb. The door is meant to be pulled open, not pushed.

Mahon's breathing and heart-rate are the same as they would be if he were sitting in a rocking chair reading a book. Beneath the blanket, he looks like a cadaver laid out for autopsy. "Right, fucking out the fucking way!"

Mahon sees the scene through the eyes of the men who have come here to do murder. They have to make up for their amateurish attempt at surprise. They have egos to massage. They have a boss to impress. And now they're standing in the cramped confines of a little wooden shed, breathing in the smell of loose compost and peat. They're taking it in. Dark in here. Seedlings in plastic trays on an ancient wooden bench at the rear. A spindle-legged wooden chair next to a shelf covered in paperbacks. A lump on the thin, uncomfortable-looking bed to their right.

"Thought you'd got away, did you?" asks the lead figure, advancing. "This is our city, you prick. No secrets from us, you prick!"

Mahon doesn't move.

The man who has spoken is slightly built. He's the youngest of the three Flemyng brothers and the one who is enjoying power the most. His name is Tyrone and he has killed two men in his short, brutish life.

"The sleep of the dead, eh, Tyrone?" says the fat, tracksuit-wearing lad behind him. His name is Bunce, and he has been Tyrone's friend since school. The third man is older and taller. He's holding bolt cutters in one hand and a large silver meat cleaver in the other. When he was younger he was the sort of boy who ate worms and broke the legs of kittens. Now he gets paid to hurt real human beings. He does it very well.

"Spear, you prick. You dead already?"

Mahon listens. A curse. The loss of temper. Two steps and then the blanket is pulled back from his face.

He opens his eyes. Lets Bunce see him for what he really is. Then he discharges the shotgun he has been holding in both hands.

Bunce's face goes through the back of his head and splatters over his companions in a vile shower of blood, skull and brains.

Mahon swings his legs off the bed and discharges the second barrel. The tall man with the cleaver slams back against the wall, holes in his torso big enough to see through.

"Spear? Fuck!"

Tyrone has forgotten that he has a gun in his coat pocket. He's too busy wiping his friend's brains from his eyes to think clearly.

Mahon hits him in the throat with the butt of the shotgun and watches him fall to his knees. He hits him again, but not hard enough to knock him out. He just wants his attention.

"I'm not Spear," he says, conversationally. "You were right to come here, in some respects. This is his dad's allotment. And I know you'd heard rumours he was back on the patch, that he was still loyal to the old boy and bad-mouthing the Flemyngs. I know that because I made sure you got to hear those stories. Spear's long gone, son. He's probably got himself a lovely tan by now. He was loyal, you were right about that. He told me lots of interesting things about the deals you were making behind Mr Nock's back. But because I'm big-hearted, I let him live. I'm not going to make you the same offer. I'm going to kill you. I'm going to kill your fucking brothers. I'm going to kill every Headhunter who even breathes in a way that Mr Nock wouldn't like."

Mahon bends down, arthritically, and picks up the shiny cleaver from the floor. He likes the look of it. Decides to think of it as his own.

"Three brothers," he says. "It never works out well. The middle child's usually the problem in families like yours. For me, it's the oldest lad that's the tricky proposition. He's the one doing the prison stretch. Hard to get to, but not impossible. Now, the middle lad shouldn't be any problem at all. I've heard that he's not as clever as you and your oldest brother, which suggests that he's on a par with some mould in a coffee cup."

Mahon pats down Tyrone, oblivious to the blood and gore that comes off on his hands. He takes his mobile phone and gun and wallet.

"You maybe didn't know that I existed," he says, looking down at the sobbing gangster. "You maybe thought I was a myth. But everything you heard is true, son. You upset Mr Nock, and his monster comes and ends your life."

Tyrone seems to shrivel inside his coat.

"Nock's dead! This is how the game is played! It's all about the game!"

Mahon shakes his head, sadly. He rubs a hand against his face and breathes in fresh blood. Eventually he nods.

"You're right," he says, crouching down and gently lifting Tyrone's chin so he can look in his eyes. "You have every right to try and take control. You have every right to hurt people and make money."

For a second, Tyrone allows a bird of hope to flutter across his face. It dies as it hits the electrified fence of Mahon's expression.

There's a gleam of light as Mahon holds the cleaver up. Its blade forms a mirror of the less devastated side of his face, and for a moment, he looks almost like a person. Then he changes the angle, and becomes a mask of nightmares made flesh.

"And I have every right to cut your fucking head off."

5

Bull Sands Prison, Mablethorpe.
Wednesday. 9.17am.

McAvoy is scrunching up his eyes like a baby who doesn't like the food in his mouth. The wind was whipping in off the sea as he walked across the car park, turning the rain and sand into tiny missiles that stung his face. Now it feels as though there is something cold and menthol covering his irises. He's forcing himself not to rub them. Has his hands pressed into his armpits, like he's wearing an invisible strait-jacket.

He opens his eyes long enough to check the time. Closes them again, hearing his heart the way others might hear a ticking clock.

According to the gadget on McAvoy's phone, this is the feast day of Saint Barbara, patron saint of artillerymen and gunsmiths, whose name should be invoked when seeking protection from lightning and fireworks. He isn't sure what to do with the information, but having viewed the clouds forming over Hull when he left this morning, he figures he may be putting in a call to Saint Babs before the day is out. He likes the idea that there is a Saint Barbara. It has a certain Yorkshire-ness to it that he finds reassuring.

McAvoy starts blinking, hoping to clear the blurriness in his vision. Winces at the sensation.

The door to the visitor suite swings open at the same moment that he realises what he must look like, hunched up and fist-faced and dripping water all over the pale blue carpet. He alters his pose. Stops as he sees the man before him. Sags a little.

There is no guard accompanying Owen. He stands there on his own, his back to the white wooden door and strands of his grey-black hair plastered across a face so thin that it looks as if the bones beneath the flesh hurt. The scar upon his forehead is a slash of white. His nose has been broken and reset. As he extends an arm, McAvoy notices that two of the fingers on his right hand point away from the others, having been inexpertly repaired.

McAvoy realises he is staring. Sorts himself out. Takes a step forward and offers his own huge hand. As he closes it around Owen's cold palm, he feels as though he is folding it over the body of a dead bird.

"Owen," he says, and it comes out too quickly. He says it again.

Owen is looking down and away: a dog that has been beaten too many times and expects nothing but more hurt. Yet there is a tension in his shoulders, as if he is holding himself in check.

"Do you want to sit down? Is anybody joining us? The officer just told me to wait here so I don't know if they're coming back or leaving us to it or what."

Owen lifts his eyes and gives a tiny nod of his head, gesturing at the door to McAvoy's rear.

"We could go for a walk," he says.

"It's grim out," says McAvoy. "Pouring down."

"I like the fresh air," says Owen, softly.

McAvoy considers his options. He doesn't yet know what Owen thinks of him and isn't sure he wants to be out on a wet, blustery day with a man who has spent four years inside because of him.

"We'll just have a seat for now," he says, and moves to one of the tables. They are laid out in rows, with plastic chairs either side. They make the portakabin look like an examination room.

"You're the boss," says Owen, and they pull up seats. McAvoy takes off his long cashmere overcoat. Underneath, he wears a grey three-piece suit and his old school tie, pulled in a perfect double-Windsor. It moves every time he swallows.

They consider one another for a moment. They look as though there should be a chess board between them.

"I'm pleased you lived," says Owen, at last. "Goes without saying, I suppose."

"You saved my life," says McAvoy, and puts a little laugh into the sentence to try and lessen the drama of it. He fails. Hears himself sounding ungrateful and churlish. A blush begins to rise up his neck.

"You're looking well," says Owen, sitting back in his chair and looking at him properly. "Nice suit. You used to be all polyester and hiking boots back in the good old days."

McAvoy twitches a smile. "My wife," he says. "Got her hands on my wardrobe and restyled me. I have no say in it."

"You look good."

"Thanks," he says, and is about to add 'so do you' when he realises how phony this would sound. He catches himself before he speaks and Owen notices.

"You're right," he says, rubbing the bridge of his broken nose. "I've seen better days."

For a moment McAvoy just listens to the sound of the waves, breaking on the shingle and sand.

"Here, I brought you something," he says, suddenly. He reaches into his jacket pocket and removes a small glass jar full of pink ointment. He puts it on the table in front of him. "I mentioned to my wife you were looking a bit tired. She made you this. You rub it under your eyes and it takes the darkness away."

Owen says nothing for a moment, though there is a half-smile playing on his lips. Then he laughs and takes the pot with a nod of thanks.

"I'd forgotten she was into that stuff," he says, sitting forward and looking a little more animated. "Lotions and potions and herbal stuff."

McAvoy nods. "She could make a career out of it, if she had the time."

"Still just the one kid?" asks Owen.

"Two now," says McAvoy. "Lilah Rose. My princess. She's coming up to three. Running me ragged."

Owen nods, looking genuinely pleased. "Still living on Kingswood?"

McAvoy is about to tell him that they have moved to a new house on Hessle Foreshore but suddenly remembers that they're not two old friends catching up over a pint in the pub. Owen has been in prison for four years because he helped McAvoy find a killer. And there's every chance that Owen has wished every kind of horror on him in return.

"We've moved," says McAvoy, clumsily. Then: "I wasn't sure you'd agree to see me."

Owen shrugs. "Not a lot I can do about it. You're a copper. You can see me whenever you decide to."

"I'm not really here as a policeman," says McAvoy, shaking his head. "Well, sort of..."

"It was a surprise, seeing you yesterday," says Owen. He seems to be ruminating on something.

"Surprise for me too."

"Good or bad?"

"Just a surprise."

They say nothing for a while. Eventually, McAvoy lets out a breath.

"I can't tell you how sorry I am," he says, willing himself to hold Owen's gaze.

Owen remains impassive. "You can try," he says, after a moment.

"I was in hospital. I was dying. By the time I got out it had already happened. You pleaded guilty."

"They told me that it was taken care of. If I pleaded

guilty to the gun possession they'd drop the other charges. I'd get a suspended sentence. It was a set-up. It was all Roper."

McAvoy feels an urge to flinch at the mention of the man who betrayed them both. Fights with himself to keep his voice steady.

"He never had that kind of power."

"Did then. Does now."

"He was a corrupt cop but he's not a cop anymore. He's gone."

Owen's nose wrinkles, as though he can smell something vile. "Gone, is he?"

"He's in London now. Consultant for some security firm. Lives the good life but he hasn't got a warrant card. We got rid of him."

Owen looks at him and through him. Shakes his head.

"That's what you tell yourself, is it?"

"That's the truth."

Owen's posture changes. The tension in his shoulders takes hold of his entire body. To McAvoy's horror, a tear runs from the corner of his eye and drops on the collar of his prison-issue T-shirt.

"Four years, Aector," he says, his voice a tremble. "Two of them in Lincoln, getting the shit kicked out of me every time my bones healed. A year in Durham, stuck among the rapists and the child-molesters, sharing a cell with a man who told me every night I'd be dead by morning. And then here, where I'm supposed to be getting rehabilitated and preparing for life back on the outside. What life? She's gone! My career's gone. The house is gone..."

"You can get it all back," begins McAvoy, hating the feebleness of the platitude.

"He did this to me," says Owen, spraying spit. "Roper. He promised me he'd do it too. Told me that once I got inside he would use all the influence he had to make sure that I bled each and every day."

McAvoy is so consumed with guilt that he feels sickness in his belly.

"I should have come before now," he says, mumbling into his shirt collar. "I'm so sorry."

Owen throws himself back in his chair. He looks as though he wants to kick the table but his eyes flick up to the camera on the wall behind McAvoy and he reins in his temper.

"Why did you come, anyway? Was it just so that every copper-hating bastard on the wing could see me being helpful with your enquiries? Did you want to make life that little bit more difficult?"

McAvoy pauses. He'd been unsure whether to wait for regular visiting hours and approach the prison as a civilian. But that was days away. He phoned the prison yesterday evening, while Pharaoh was pulling strings with Lincolnshire Police, the Coroner's Office and the Health and Safety Executive to get hold of all the reports into Will Blaylock's death. He arranged to speak to Prisoner HN 8761 first thing in the morning. Set off at 7.30, having held Roisin hard enough to squeeze the air from her lungs. Be careful, she said. Let him say what he needs to. Don't let him make you hate yourself...

McAvoy pushes a hand through his hair, pulls out his phone and flicks through the emails in his inbox until he finds the photographs. Looks at the shot of William Blaylock lying on the floor of a farm building: limbs like a swastika; his entire trunk a mess of bone and flesh. He looks at the image as if to remind himself. Puts the phone down on the table, face down.

"William Blaylock," says McAvoy. "I got the impression he was your friend."

Owen looks at the back of the phone like a gambler trying to read an opponent's cards.

"His inquest was yesterday. Accidental death. Nobody to blame. You're too late. Again."

"I thought that might not be your opinion," says McAvoy, quietly.

"I'm a convicted criminal. My opinion doesn't matter."

McAvoy gives it a moment. Feels his temperature rising.

"If my boss was here she'd be getting sick of you playing silly buggers right about now."

"Shame she's not," says Owen, rudely. "Pharaoh, isn't it? I

knew her when she was a DCI. Tasty. Hard. Can't imagine you two are the best of friends."

"Think what you like," says McAvoy, allowing the first stirrings of temper to show in his face. "I came here to help you. I can go."

"You came here because you feel guilty," says Owen, jaw locked. "You thought you'd put a bad memory to bed and then yesterday you ran slap-bang into me. And because you're a decent bloke it all came flooding back. And you wondered if there was any way on earth you could make it up to me. So you pulled Will's file and convinced that great ginger head of yours that you could atone for leaving me to rot by getting some justice for Will. But you know what, Aector? Life isn't like that. And the thing I want you to take away from today is that the only person who has surprised me in my whole cynical fucking life, is you. I knew Roper would make my life hell. I knew deep down Tony had something wrong with him. But I never thought you would leave me here. I never thought it would take you four years."

McAvoy wants to press his hand to his own chest. He can feel his heart thumping inside him.

"I couldn't," he says, wheezy and indistinct. "I couldn't even think about what happened without my legs giving way. It took every ounce of strength to get myself back to work. And a year after that somebody tried to kill me in those same damn woods. I just couldn't."

Owen looks at him. Keeps the snarl on his face, even as his eyes soften. He slows his breathing. Reaches forward and flips over McAvoy's phone. He closes his eyes after a moment. "What makes you think there's more to it than the official verdict?" he asks, in little more than a whisper. "Seriously. I know you want to make things right between us but put that aside. Tell me what you're thinking."

McAvoy rubs his eyes. Tries to get himself together.

"It seems to have been sorted too quickly," he says, thinking aloud. "Dead in the summer, inquest tied up at the beginning of December? No real cross-examination of witnesses. No real explanation what he was doing with the auger."

"You know what they are?"

"I grew up on a croft. My dad looked at manuals of farming equipment the way most people look at pornography. Yes, I know what they are. I know you can get dragged into them by your hair or your shoelaces or by loose-fitting clothes but unless you're juggling with them it's damn hard to drive them through your chest."

Owen is looking at McAvoy curiously. His pupils are pin-pricks.

"He didn't deserve what happened to him."

"You were there."

"I held him."

"As he died?"

"He was long gone."

"You raised the alarm?"

"I shouted. Two of the farm-hands came. They went running and brought the boss. He saw what had happened and went to phone an ambulance."

"He went away to do that?"

"No phone signal in the outbuilding. Had to go and use the landline."

McAvoy nods. The register of calls is among the documents mailed to him late last night.

"Tell me about Will," he says, picking up the phone and looking again at the boy's ruined body.

"We were room-mates at first," says Owen, sighing. "He was an okay lad. Bit out of his depth, but I could sympathise with that. I'm sure the Hull Mail will say he was this terrible specimen but he wasn't like you think. He dealt, yeah, but to his friends. It was mostly cannabis. His mum had arthritis and he got into growing it for her. Sold some extra to help pay the bills. He did a year of university before he made the mistake of thinking he'd found himself a more lucrative career. He started supplying people who were much worse than him and he got busted the second a half-decent copper heard about his operation. He confessed the lot. He did eight months in Nottingham before coming here and we were roomed together. He was a clever lad. We've got a quiz team, me and some of the other thinkers. He was good company. Funny."

McAvoy sees genuine warmth in Owen's eyes as he talks about the young lad. He keeps his questions gentle.

"He took work on the farm?"

"He liked the outdoors. The prison used to have its own farm on site but there are temporary cell-blocks there now because of overcrowding. That meant the authorities needed to find somewhere inmates could work. The old boy at Gilberdyke seemed a neat fit. Prisoners go there in a bus in the morning and come back at night. Same arrangement at four other farms, a bit closer to here."

McAvoy tries not to let his surprise show. Every time he thinks about prisoners being allowed to hold down jobs and earn money and then go back to their prisons for a movie and bed, he wonders if there is any point to his job. Then he talks himself round. He understands the need for rehabilitation; abhors the idea of people being left in cells to rot. It always troubles him that his first instinct is so different to the opinion he holds after three seconds of rational thought.

"You worked the farm too?"

"First three months at an open prison you don't leave the site. Then you can be considered for work outside. I worked in the Sentence Management Unit at first, getting files ready and making cups of tea and stuff. Pretty okay."

"But you ended up on the farm?"

Owen looks away. "Contraband found in my cell. I lost privileges. Nearly got shipped back to Lincoln."

"What was the contraband?" asks McAvoy.

Owen gives a little laugh. "Herbs," he says, softly.

"Herbs? You mean cannabis?"

"No, I mean fucking herbs."

McAvoy raises his eyebrows, waiting for more.

"Will was into all that herb stuff, like your missus. It was meant to be a nice gesture. I swapped a couple of phone cards with one of the kitchen staff and they added some extras to the weekly order. Dill. Lemongrass. Speedwell. Thyme. They were found in my cell. I ended up on the farm, picking bloody

sprouts and turnips and sweating so much I thought I was
going to die."

McAvoy isn't sure what to say so he starts flicking through
the files in his phone. He finds the inventory of Will's possessions, cleared from his cell after 200-plus inmates helped themselves to the bits they fancied. A few photographs of family
members. A desk globe that doubled as a pencil sharpener. A
bottle of Sarson's vinegar. Four pairs of socks. A flyer for a
comedy night, signed by the comedian. A box of pencils and a
sketch pad containing no sketches.

McAvoy looks back up. Owen is staring at him, wet-eyed
and white-faced.

"He wasn't sharing his cell with you at the end," says
McAvoy, reading the report.

Owen shakes his head. "He was moved after a month or so.
In with another couple of lads."

"I can't see their names," says McAvoy, looking again at his
screen.

"Spear," says Owen, blankly. "Kremlin. They both slept with
one eye open but it didn't do Kremlin any good."

"Mitchell Spear?" asks McAvoy, carefully.

"Yeah. Released on licence last summer and hasn't been
seen since."

"Why did he move cells?"

"I told you," says Owen, looking away. "People like to play
with my head."

"And Kremlin?"

"Real name Flemyng. Heir to the throne, or so he thought."

McAvoy sees the way Owen's eyes twitch and shift, glancing
at the door and over the bigger man's shoulder. He wonders if
he has any right to accuse the man of being paranoid after so
many years and so many beatings.

"You're saying he was moved because you were his friend?"

Owen shrugs. "It was a shame. We were getting on. But we
still hung out. He was still in the quiz team."

McAvoy looks confused. "Who do you actually play?"

"The guards. Other prisons. It's taken pretty seriously."

"I've never heard of that."

"Why would you? This is a prison. There's a rock band and a badminton league and a pool table and if that got in the Daily Mail it would mean headaches for the governor."

"He was clever?"

"For a young lad," nods Owen.

"Too clever to start playing about with an auger he didn't know how to operate?"

Owen gives a gesture somewhere between a nod and a shrug. He looks suddenly tired. Takes the pot of ointment and starts passing it from hand to hand.

"How did he find his new cellmates?" asks McAvoy, as the wheels in his mind begin to turn. "Were they into the same things he was?"

"The hippy stuff? No chance. But he knew his stuff. If you asked him nicely he'd tell you what your alternative sign was."

"Alternative sign?"

"Yeah, like whether you were a hazel or an oak or a birch. He knew which plants were good when your back was sore. Told me once that if you rubbed a red chilli against a red candle and stroked it from base to top, it would get anybody who breathed it in in the mood for love. You can imagine how most of the lads in here would respond to that."

McAvoy wonders if he should ask whether there was anything more between Owen and Will than friendship. Even as he decides not to, Owen reads it in his eyes.

"Not guilty, your honour," he says, smiling. "Even after four years I can't say I'm tempted. And neither was he. Nothing against those who are, it's just not for me."

McAvoy isn't sure what to do with the information so he goes back to playing with his phone. Outside, the wind is picking up and it feels as the portakabin is shaking on its foundations.

"Imagine if we took off," says Owen. "You and me, whizzing through the air like Dorothy and Toto. Let's hope to Christ we land on Roper, eh?"

The two men share their first genuine smile in four years. It feels nice. They were never exactly friends but they liked one another, back before it all went wrong. They would exchange knowing looks at police press conferences and McAvoy liked the funny little texts Owen used to send when the press pack were waiting at crime scenes for progress reports. It was McAvoy Owen turned to when he found himself accused of attacking a young woman operating on Doug Roper's instructions. It was Owen McAvoy approached when he made his discoveries about Tony Halthwaite. If not for all the blood, they could have become close.

"You're really going to make some enquiries?" asks Owen.

"Do you think I should?"

Owen sits for a long moment. He lets his eyes flick to the camera in the corner of the room. He hunches forward, body language changing.

"That camera's recording us, Aector. It's got pictures but no sound. If I'm seen helping you then my life gets fucking worse. There's so much I want to tell you. So much you should know but you don't. Thing is, everybody in here does know. If you put half a dozen ex-convicts in charge of the police force you'd soon solve every single crime. We all know what happened to Will. But it will happen to me if I help you. Everything you need's in your reports if you read between the lines."

"Was he murdered, Owen?"

Owen sighs. "You haven't got a clue. I don't know what to make of you. Never bloody have."

"I was going to go to the scene," gabbles McAvoy, as he senses Owen preparing to leave. "To speak to the farmer."

Owen gives a slight nod. Looks at McAvoy with something in his eyes that might be pity.

"You ever skip?" he asks, out of nowhere. "Remember those old playground chants. Salt, pepper, vinegar, mustard. I've had the song stuck in my head since before he died. It won't leave. Keeps the spirits away, eh? You should ask your wife."

McAvoy opens his hands, seeking more.

"They took what they wanted from his cell when he was gone," says Owen, quietly. "Nothing that mattered was there anyway."

"He kept his treasured possessions with you?"

"What treasured possessions?"

"I don't know. Wallet. Drawings or whatever."

"You think my cell is safer?" asks Owen. He sits forward suddenly. His shirt falls open. A long brown cord hangs around his neck, disappearing into his shirt. As he moves, McAvoy spots the pendant at the end. It is a paperclip, bent to form a shape he does not recognise. It looks like a lower case 'm', with a hanging tail.

"I can't give you any more," says Owen. "The coroner didn't even mention his arms, for Christ's sake. I'm sorry all this had to happen. I didn't mean to get you involved."

"The herbs," says McAvoy, struggling to keep up. "You took the blame. They were his..."

"Salt, pepper, vinegar, mustard. Lovely Speedwell. Ask your wife."

"I don't understand."

"I'm sorry," says Owen, flicking a glance at the video camera. "They're watching."

Before McAvoy can speak again, Owen lunges forward and grabs him by his collar with both hands. Instinctively, he pulls back and Owen is dragged across the table, hissing pure hatred in his face. The door bangs open and three men in white shirts and blue ties rush forward and grab Owen. As he struggles to disentangle himself, McAvoy sees one of the men strike Owen hard in the face with his knee. He pulls himself upright, half compelled to pull the prison officers from his former friend, but something in Owen's eyes holds him where he stands

"Hold his arms," shouts one of the guards, as another tells McAvoy that the interview is over.

"You can't put this right," spits Owen, eyes locked on McAvoy's. "I ain't saying a fucking thing."

McAvoy is left standing there as they bundle Owen back out of the door and into the gale.

Standing, looking up at the camera, and wondering how much was performance and how much pure, white-hot hate.

6

The roses are Lithuanian. They are an entirely new variety and look as if they are made up of limitless folds of white and pink silk. Their thorns are over an inch long. They are the centrepieces of a dozen different bouquets, strategically placed around the houseboat so that their recipient can see them in whichever direction she's looking. Some of the bouquets contain lilies, and that is the scent she can smell now, even above the aroma of the skin lotion she rubs into her hips and thighs while considering herself in the full-length mirror.

"*Lankininkas siela*," he had whispered in her ear, both hands over her eyes and steering her down the stairs and through the door. "*Archer Soul*. Named for you. So's the boat, though on paper you'll have to change your name to MV Endless Summer."

The dress she was wearing is ruined. One of the bunches of flowers got knocked over during their lovemaking and a splatter of red pollen from the lilies is smeared across the front.

Detective Chief Inspector Sharon Archer pulls the silk robe from the hook on the back of the bathroom door and enjoys the sensation of it on her damp skin. She rubs mist from the mirror and checks her teeth. She has them expensively whitened every three months. Has herself Botoxed every six. Has her eyebrows plucked by an Indian girl using twists of thread. She wonders if she should put on some make-up, but decides that the man in the bedroom next door will not appreciate it. He is happy to stand the cost of her beautification treatments but will not be pleased at being kept waiting while she applies lipstick and foundation, mascara and creams, just for it to be rubbed off on the Egyptian cotton sheets as he pushes her face into the bed with his firm, unyielding hands.

Satisfied, she turns away from the glass. She catches the smell of lilies again and wonders what it is about the scent that disquiets her Archer hears her name being called and realises she has been standing still, staring into nothing, lost in memories. She can smell those bloody lilies again. They remind her of something she can't place.

She shakes herself a little. Pulls open the bathroom door and steps out, smiling.

"Lovely," he says, nodding. "You put the roses to shame."

He's lying on rumpled white sheets, unashamedly naked. An ashtray rests on his chest and he is smoking a long, white cigarette with a gold band around the filter. In the bedroom, the smell of lilies competes with the scent of menthol and nicotine, freshly-brewed coffee and their shared sweat.

"Don't know why you showered," he says, looking at her with a half-smile. "I'm going to mess you up again."

"I thought I'd give you a blank canvas to paint on," she says, standing at the foot of the bed. She knows from experience not to lie down upon it until invited to do so. Even taking a shower could have been viewed as an act of defiance.

"You left your phone out," he says, nodding at the white-painted dresser. On it sit expensive lotions and perfumes. Her phone is where she left it.

Archer's stomach knots. She does a quick mental scan of anything incriminating she may have left undeleted in her phone. Can think of nothing, but knows that may not matter.

"Did you look?" she asks.

He smiles at her, the cigarette clamped between his small, white teeth.

"Do I need to?"

"No," she says, feeling her face begin to colour.

"Why's that, Sherilyn?"

She tries to hold his gaze and admits defeat. "Because you know everything anyway."

"So why would I mind you leaving your phone out?"

Archer pulls on her earlobe while she thinks how best to answer. She wears no earrings when she sees him. He likes to pull her hair and doesn't care whether her jewels are ripped from her lobes when he does so.

"The battery," she says.

He looks at her like a proud parent. "Well done, my darling. You win a kiss."

Meekly, Archer moves around the bed and stands beside him. He reaches up and takes the silk of her robe and drags her forward. She resists for only a second. He has soft lips and they press against hers tenderly. She feels his hand slip inside her robe and she goes stiff in his embrace as she feels the stinging pain upon her taut, tanned stomach. He looks into her eyes while he presses the tip of the cigarette against her belly.

"You take the battery out," he says, not unkindly. "You take the battery out and then it can't be traced. Or you leave it the fuck at home. Or you throw it in the river. I've told you this before. The fact that you've disobeyed me suggests that you don't respect me. And that doesn't make me feel happy. You want me to feel happy, don't you?"

There are tears in Archer's eyes, but she refuses to look away. She can smell her skin cooking.

"Are we going to let this spoil today?" he asks, cocking his head.

"No," says Archer.

"Promise?"

She pushes forward. Kisses him. Both their eyes are open and she sees his lenses and his dark irises blend together and multiply, as though she is kissing him through a cracked mirror. She feels the cigarette lift from her skin. He indicates that she should climb over him onto the bed. She does so, trying not to show any pain. He reaches down and takes a melting ice-cube from the silver chiller on the hardwood floor and passes it to her. She applies it to her burn while he relights his slightly crumpled cigarette with his lighter. It's a Ronson. He told her once it was a special edition; a replica of the one used by James Bond in Casino Royale. He hadn't told her to impress her. Just thought she might be interested. If Archer were honest with herself, she would admit that the man next to her couldn't give a damn whether she is impressed or not. He bought her this houseboat, moored at South Dock Marina in Southwark, and filled it with a new variety of lilies, because he likes the way such acts make him feel about himself. It should have cost £600,000, but the previous owner was persuaded to settle more cheaply for cash. It has two bedrooms and for the past month, a team of decorators have been turning it into a palatial extravaganza of whites, creams and natural wood. It's so damn tasteful that Archer feels as though she is being pressed between the pages of a glossy magazine. Of course, the gift comes at a price. She has no doubt that he will fuck his whores here. Has no doubt he will ensure that the same dirty sheets are laid out upon the bed next time she comes to London. He'll probably tell her, in her moments of ecstasy, that the scent in her nostrils is the sweat of an Albanian teenager he abused while she was driving down. She will cry because he likes it, and then she will climax all the harder.

Archer lets the ice melt against her skin. Enjoys the cooling sensation almost as much as part of her liked the burn.

"I love the boat," she says, drawing her legs up and inspecting the red nail varnish on her toes. As she does so, her robe falls open, and her lover smirks a little as he glimpses her nakedness beneath.

"I knew you would," he says. "You don't have to worry about it. It's registered in the company name but it's yours. Yours, as much as anything is. Yours, the way you're mine."

Archer nods and looks away. On paper, she is three different people. One of those people is Antonia Snow. She is the owner of a string of nail salons and beauty parlours across South London and last year, they had a turnover in excess of eight million pounds. The business cleans up some of her lover's money. She is rarely needed for anything more elaborate than an appearance at the bank to sign paperwork. For that, she receives a quarterly dividend worth five times her police salary. On top of that, she has received gifts of racehorses, stud ponies, a Porsche Boxster and a houseboat. Were any of it traceable, she would be subject to an internal police enquiry that would land her in prison until she was an old lady. But her lover covers his tracks very well. And besides, were anybody to know the truth about the person she is when not catching criminals, her lover would put them in the ground.

She is about to say something appropriately grateful when she is again assailed by the smell of lilies. Suddenly she remembers. While a Detective Sergeant in Newcastle, she was hurt while apprehending an armed robber during an early morning house raid. She ended up in hospital, with a compacted vertebrae at the top of her spine. She received gifts of chocolate and wine, teddies and cards. Her boss sent lilies, addressed to the Hunchback of Notre Dame. She smiled upon receiving them, remembering the look on his ratty face as she told him that her school had been named after the French cathedral. He always made her smile. He respected her tenacity and brains. She was nearly twenty years younger than him but they became something akin to best friends. They moved to Humberside Police together. His name was Detective Chief Inspector Colin Ray and a few months ago he learned her secret. She has never asked her lover what he did with him. Doesn't think she could stand to find out.

"Did I tell you the roses are Lithuanian?" he asks, nodding at the vase on the antique steamer trunk at the foot of the bed. "Best in the world. Ask anybody."

"They're beautiful," she says.

He looks away, content with himself.

Archer wonders if she could call what she feels for him 'love'. In her heart, she considers the word too anodyne to suffice. Love makes her think of flimsy, flighty people who need endless reassurance and who pop one another's spots. What she feels for him is something else. He speaks to a part of her that she used to be ashamed of. He is a violent and dangerous man. She knew who he was when she let him seduce her. She did not know the scale of his ambition but she knew he was very, very bad. It didn't stop her growing so infatuated with him that when he told her to fuck one of his business associates, she did it without question. She did not set out to be corrupted. That part of her was already there. By the time she was taking money to lose evidence and scare off witnesses for his criminal associates, she was well past the point of analysing her motives. She has no get-out plan. She does not know what she will say if she is ever found out. She simply cannot imagine such a possibility. He is too much in control for that. And from what she can tell, he has dirt on everybody with the power to hurt him.

Archer reaches out and touches the ink upon his shoulder. The face of the devil, skull-like and leering, is staring at her with an expression of both pleasure and pain. An upturned spider squats like a dead hand upon the washboard of his stomach. He has Cyrillic stars tattooed upon his pectoral muscles and knees. Archer knows what they say about this man. Knows what it says about her that she would kill for him in a moment.

He wraps his hands around hers. Brushes the hair back from her face. He is moving down the bed; gliding over the luxurious cotton. She knows where he is going. He wants to put his tongue upon her burned skin. Wants to taste her, but wants to get the angle right, so he can watch himself do it in the mirror.

Archer gives a small huff of disappointment as his phone begins to ring. Quick and business-like, he stands up and finds his phone.

He stands, naked, admiring himself in the mirror. He answers the phone with a curt "Privet".

She watches him as he listens. Nothing changes in his face but his eyes darken. He reaches forward and plucks the head off one of the roses, crushes it in his palm as he talks, swiftly and quietly. He rattles off a number. Gives a name. Hangs up with a promise that he will be there soon.

On the bed Archer watches him get dressed. He seems to have forgotten she is there. As he slips on his jacket, he looks at her with eyes that are made blacker by the brilliant white of the wall he is standing against.

"He's been to see Swainson," he says, quietly, rolling the word on his tongue like brandy.

Archer's mind races. Shock shows in her face as she remembers what the name means. Realises, too, who 'he' must be.

"What did they say to each other?" she asks, gathering her robe around herself as if somebody is watching.

He shakes his head. Smiles, as if making a decision.

"Maybe time to stop playing with him," he says. "He should have been underground years ago. It was indulgence to let him live."

"He deserved to suffer," says Archer, dutifully, pulling herself onto her knees and looking at him the way a dog would look at its master.

"Bet they had a lot to talk about," he says, staring at the wall and ignoring Archer. "Fuck, that Jock bastard gets everywhere."

"What can I do?"

In this moment, Archer knows that she is entirely his to command. She doesn't give a damn about domination, or empowerment, or the bullshit people tell themselves when they realise they're not sufficiently in love to give or take the odd beating. She would rather be who she is than any of the poor, enfeebled victims who get the shit kicked out of them each Friday and Saturday night by men they weren't good enough to please. Archer always despised them, even as she was arresting their abusers. She lets this man hurt her because she likes it.

"The inquest," she says, remembering. "We dealt with that, didn't we? Accidental death, no more problems..."

He holds up his hand to shush her. Runs his hand down the inside of her bare leg to her perfect toes. She trembles as he plays with them, unsure if she will receive a kiss or if he will produce hedge-clippers and snip one off. It is a feeling she knows, and needs.

"It's in hand," he says, rubbing his thumb against the pad of her big toe. "He knows better than to say anything. We own him."

"But he's never told you ..."

He twists his hand, sudden and violent, and Archer cries out in pain as he dislocates her second smallest toe.

He stands up, looking down on her as she whimpers on the bed, clutching her aching foot.

"He'll tell me now," he says, half to her and half to himself. "The fucker will tell me as he dies."

Archer watches him leave and hopes to God that by the time he is back in her bed, he will have forgiven her for daring to question him.

Above all, she hopes he will not mind if she gathers up the lilies and throws them into the sea. She cannot stand the memories, the realisation that she misses her old friend.

Painfully, she slides across the bed and retrieves her phone from the dresser. For a moment she looks through the windows at the purple sky above the docks. Marvels at the blackness of the water and the daffodil yellow of the lamps that light the quay.

Finds herself smiling, through the pain. He'll come back. In his own way, he loves her. In his own way, he thinks of her as the only person with whom he can be entirely himself.

She knows who he is, who he was, and who he intends to be.

It is four years since he was Detective Superintendent Doug Roper. Three years since he established a consultancy firm in London and began offering security solutions to outfits of questionable morality. For the last couple of years, that company has been little more than a front for a criminal organisation that the authorities call the Headhunters, which has left burned bodies up and down the country and changed the nature of organised crime.

She is his lover. And she will take all the pain he wants to dish out.

7

W hat little sunshine the day had brought is bleeding into darkness by the time McAvoy spots the sudden gap in the hedgerows to his right and swings the car onto a rutted farm-track. Through the dirty streaks on the windscreen and the half-hearted rain that blows in from the river, he can make out the distant shape of the main farmhouse. It does not look inviting. He grudgingly lets go of his vague fantasy that some rosy-cheeked farmer's wife will come out to greet him with a tray of fresh-baked scones, a pot of tea, and offers of a complimentary shoulder rub.

He's driven with his headlights on all day but in this bruised half-light he feels a sudden urge to flick them to full-beam. He slows down to double check he is in the right place. The sat-nav function in his phone confirms he has found Shepton Farm, though he is feeling sufficiently harassed to think that he would have had more success if he had typed "arse end of nowhere" into the address box.

For the past hour he has been teaching the sat-nav a variety of new words, cursing it in English, Gaelic and something unintelligible as it repeatedly lost the signal and left him adrift, performing complicated u-turns on single-track roads as he did battle with the landscape, lost in a two-mile stretch of countryside between Newport and Gilberdyke.

He takes a breath and enjoys the fleeting sensation of victory. He widens his eyes as he looks at himself in the rearview mirror, gesturing at his own reflection the way he would to a friend; a wordless camaraderie, as if in acknowledgement that the afternoon has been more demanding than it should have been.

He winds down the window and sticks his head out, examining the road. It's in poor repair and the last of the snow has been turned into muddy slush by vehicles with tyres the width of tree trunks. He can smell the familiar tang of turnips and livestock, fuel and wet earth. He knows from his notes that Shepton Farm is a big operation but apart from the distant hum of a generator, it looks quiet now. There are a few lights on in an outbuilding beyond the main house and he can make out the glare of a single bulb shining above what he takes to be the front door. He moves the car forward and the farm comes into focus. It's an impressive structure: Grade II listed and two hundred years old. It's long, rectangular, a double door in the centre of what would have been the original building. Two large bay windows protrude either side. The farmhouse has been extended since it was first constructed and McAvoy can see a long, one-storey building running away towards the treeline. It is the largest of the buildings on the satellite images that McAvoy had called up on his laptop in a Starbucks at a motorway service station, while talking through his meeting with Owen with the two women in his life. There is a modern, three-bedroom house around a quarter of a mile from the main house and the space in between is taken up with covered outbuildings and cattle sheds. The property is bordered on all sides by quality arable land, though it still looks more like the dairy farm it used to be.

With the house on his right, McAvpy heads for a courtyard area lit by large halogen spotlights. He feels a moment's uncertainty. It could almost be called fear. He does not chide himself for it. He has spent too much time alone in the dark, facing people who wish him harm, not to experience disquiet at situations that resonate on that same sinister frequency. He remembers his promise to Pharaoh and Roisin that he would be careful.. McAvoy still hasn't processed his thoughts about the meeting with Owen. He thought, for a moment, that Owen wanted him to proceed; to look further into the death of his young friend. But then his temper frayed and he spit such bile upon him that McAvoy half expected the other man's saliva to start eating through his clothes. As he drove away, hands gripping the steering wheel too tightly, he hadn't known what to do next. Should he walk away? What did Owen actually want him to do? As he went north, he started to think a little more rationally. Owen needed to protect himself. When he lunged across the table it was for the benefit of the camera and the guards. Perhaps that was the reason he was so cryptic. What had he said that might have had two meanings? Stuff about herbs and condiments. Horoscopes. Something about the dead man's arms and asking Roisin.

McAvoy hits the brakes as he pulls into the forecourt, jerking forward in his seat. A large, battered Toyota Hi-Lux is blocking his path, parked at an angle across the road. Through the open window, McAvoy can hear the hum of a generator and the sound of raised voices.

McAvoy opens his car door and climbs out. His foot goes straight into a puddle of dirty water. Cursing, he hops forward, reaching into his pocket for his warrant card as he makes his way past the parked car. He raises a hand to shield his eyes from the glare of the lights, and stops short as he looks at the scene before him. A large man with a completely bald head has his fists around the overalls of a middle-aged man. They are almost nose to nose and the bigger man is baring his teeth, eyes bulging, spit on his chin. On the floor is an older man. One wellington boot has come off as he fell backwards and it sticks out of the mud, comically, as he flounders, trying to pull himself up using the metal sides of a wheelbarrow full of plastic bags.

"Humberside Police," says McAvoy, instinctively. "Let go of him."

The big man turns to McAvoy with a glare. "Fuck off, copper. I'm gonna bite his fucking eyes out."

"No, you're not," says McAvoy, taking a step forward and reaching into his long coat. In his pocket is his asp, the extendable baton that can prove lethal in the hands of a man of McAvoy's size, and which he has never allowed himself to use.

"Get off me," squeals the man being held by his clothes. "Just take your stuff and go.!"

The big man looks McAvoy up and down. McAvoy can see him weighing it up. He seems the sort of man who would love to hurt a copper, but when the copper in question looks like McAvoy, there may be merit in strategic retreat.

A sudden honk from the parked car causes McAvoy to jump and the noise snaps the tension. The big man pushes the man in overalls down to the ground and steps over his sprawled frame. He grabs two black bin-liners from the wheelbarrow and turns his back on the two men.

"Where do you think you're going?" asks McAvoy, shocked at his brazenness. "You just carried out an assault in full view of an officer of Humberside Police."

"Leave it," comes a small voice to McAvoy's right. The older man is pulling himself up, mud on his face and clothes. "It was just a bit of fun. No harm done."

The big man looks at McAvoy and winks. McAvoy would put his age at early forties. There is a large tattoo on his neck of some kind of demonic creature, which is considerably more attractive than the face of the man himself. He has waxy, fleshy cheeks and a chipped front tooth, frog-like eyes and a mouth that doesn't shut all the way.

"See, officer," says the man. "No problems."

McAvoy wants to stop him but isn't sure what he can really do. The victims look as if they don't want any more trouble and while McAvoy is willing to try and restrain him, he has no idea how many other passengers there may be in the car.

"What's your name?" asks McAvoy, fixing him with a hard look.

"What's yours?" ask the big man, through a smile.

"Detective Sergeant Aector McAvoy," says McAvoy, and instantly realises he only admitted this because he didn't want to be seen to back down.

"I'll remember that," says the big man.

"Is that a threat?" asks McAvoy, cocking his head.

"Couldn't threaten a police officer," the big man says. "That would be naughty. See you when I see you."

McAvoy holds his ground and the man walks past him and climbs into the driver's seat of the car. McAvoy makes a mental note of the number plate. As the car's headlights blaze into life, he gets a glance at the passenger. He's shorter. Younger. Probably no more than twenty-five. He's looking at McAvoy curiously, eyebrows furrowed. He has his chair pushed back as far as it will go. In the moment before the car pulls away, McAvoy clocks the black band and plastic face of an electronic tag strapped to his ankle.

McAvoy hears a thunk of metal on metal as the HiLux reverses out of the courtyard and clips the side of his own car. He winces and gives a half-hearted "hey" but another dint in his battered people-carrier doesn't seem to matter. He turns to the two men, opening his hands in a way that suggest he wants answers, now.

"It was nothing," says the older man as he tries to get his foot back into his Wellington boot, supporting his weight on the other man's shoulder, who looks at McAvoy with an expression somewhere between defiance and relief.

"What the hell was all that?" asks McAvoy. "More importantly, who was it?"

The older man seems to gather himself a little. He's in his sixties. He looks like he was a big guy once but age has withered him. His thin, grey hair has receded back to the crown and there are patches of grey and specks of red on his upper lip and chin that suggest difficulty with his morning shave. There is a wateriness to his eyes. He is wrapped up against the cold wind which swirls around him and whips up tiny peaks on the surfaces of the dirty puddles.

"Ron Erskine," says the man, extending his left hand and

withdrawing it again when he sees how dirty it is. "This is my place. Don't trouble yourself, officer. Just a bit of argy-bargy."

McAvoy lets his feelings show. "Argy bargy? He looked like he would have bitten your face off!" He turns to the other man. "Your name, sir?"

This man is in his thirties. He's not actually all that small. He just appeared so next to his attacker. He's got a broad chest and large forearms and big, broken hands. He flashes a look at Erskine, who gives a tired nod of assent.

"Dan Prince. Foreman. Blokes call me Goalpost, if that matters." He gives a little shake of his head, aware he's rambling. "Thanks for that. He's a big bugger." He looks at McAvoy, up and further up. "So are you. Honestly, it was nothing."

McAvoy glares at the pair of them, knowing they have decided on their story and are sticking to it. He pinches the bridge of his nose and breathes out.

"My name's McAvoy," he says, treating the one fact he is sure about like a lifejacket. "I'm with the Serious and Organised Unit within Humberside Police. As part of our enquiries, we have a few extra little questions about the death of William Blaylock. Nothing major but any help you can give me would be appreciated."

Erskine and Prince both suddenly look like children who have just been told that instead of going to Disneyland, they're going to spend a fortnight getting hosed down in a cellar.

"That's done!" says Erskine, aghast. "The inquest was yesterday. All sorted. I wasn't to blame. That's done!"

"It's been hard," says Prince, nodding at his boss. "Can't we just let it go?"

As they continue their protestations, McAvoy leans forward and looks into the wheelbarrow. When the big man lifted out the bin liners, some of the contents spilled out. In the half-light, McAvoy makes out a bottle of nail varnish and a small, clear vial of what looks like anti-bacterial hand-sanitizer.

Erskine sees him looking and manoeuvres his body between McAvoy and the wheelbarrow. He gives a mollifying shrug, sagging a little.

"Sorry, sorry, I know you're just doing your job. Look, this has been shit, y'know? I had to pay for a solicitor in case anything was said about it being my fault. Felt like a weight had been lifted. It's done, isn't it? You're not re-opening it or something."

McAvoy feels a wave of pity for him. He softens his face. "Mr Erskine, we just want to get to the bottom of certain matters. Mr Blaylock's name has come up in in connection with other investigations and I am trying to tick a few boxes to show we've done things right."

McAvoy isn't sure if he's telling the truth but decides not to analyse his words too carefully in case he finds out he is lying. He nods at the wheelbarrow. Tries to lighten the mood.

"Not your shade, I wouldn't have thought."

Erskine looks confused. "Sorry?"

"The nail varnish. Thought it should be Farmer green."

Erskine twitches a grin. It sits there, false and forced. "Just clearing out the Ponderosa," he says, and something flickers in his face as he says it. "The Lodge, like."

McAvoy wonders if he should press him, whether the man he saw is an aggrieved husband who has unearthed some kind of affair between his partner and Prince or Erskine. He feels almost relieved to have a theory.

"What is it you need?" asks Prince, rubbing dry mud off his hands.

"I've seen your statements about the day Mr Blaylock died. Is there anything you wish to add?"

"Like what?" asks Erskine.

"I'm just a little perturbed by how the auger got him where it did."

Erskine looks exasperated, as if he has been over this too many times. "It was just pure bad luck. He shouldn't have been in the building with the power tools in the first place but I'm too soft for my own good. So's Dan. We've never had any bother with the inmates. They're good workers. Good lads, though you can't help wondering what they're in for. We get some rough buggers out here but the lads from the prison are more grateful for the job than the students and halfwits we used to get through the agency. Cheaper, too. Don't know where we'd be without them."

"Quiet here today," says McAvoy, looking at his watch. "Not even five."

"Not much to be doing," shrugs Prince. "December's a quiet month. We still have a few dropped off by the prison bus but they help me on a bit of upkeep and general maintenance rather than planting or picking. We did sprouts last year. You should have seen the place last December. Bloody manic it was. Didn't plant them this year. Good decision."

"The building where the incident occurred," says McAvoy. "That's some way from the main farm, yes?"

"It's a big spread," says Erskine. "I've owned it 27 years and bought four new plots in that time. 270 acres in total. Outbuildings all over."

"And why was Mr Blaylock in that particular building at that time?"

"It was a hot day. Bloody baking, to be honest. He went in to cool off. It's nice and shaded. Can't blame the lad for wanting to get out of the heat."

"So he was hiding there, effectively? Bunking off?"

Prince grins. "Boys will be boys."

"And then he, what, just picked up an enormous drilling machine and started playing with it?"

"We think he'd seen me using it," says Prince, a little too loud. "Probably wanted to try it. It's got a hell of a kick though. Just horrible luck."

"His friend," says McAvoy. "The one who found him. He gave evidence that suggested there was some delay between his discovery and calling the emergency services."

"No mobile signal out there," says Erskine. "Had to call from the house. Wouldn't have made any difference anyway. He was long since dead."

McAvoy considers this. Looks at the two men with just enough doubt in his expression to make them feel uneasy.

"Could I see the building where it happened?"

Prince is clearly about to blurt out a reason why not, when Erskine says that yes, of course McAvoy can see it.

"Bit of a hike," says Erskine. "My old knees are bugging me but Dan can run you out, yeah?"

Prince looks less than pleased, but he does a good job of covering it up. "Wait there," he says, and turns and walks across the forecourt.

"Nice home," says McAvoy, companionably, as they wait. "Nice place to raise kids."

"Kids are all grown up," says Erskine. "Nice when they were little, though."

"You live here with your wife?"

He shakes his head. His lips become a line. "She's not so well. Early onset Alzheimer's. She's only 67. Bloody horrible illness. She's in a nice place out near York. Expensive, but she's happier there."

McAvoy closes his eyes. Such horrors terrify him. He has always had a parent's fear of the bruises on his children's legs turning out to be leukaemia, or that the headaches he suffers are signs of a growing tumour. Roisin helps him overcome such paranoia, though while he agrees with her there is no point worrying, he cannot help but think he's right to be cautious.

A moment later, Prince returns on a large quad bike. McAvoy has to fight against the grin that threatens to explode. He hasn't been on a quad for years. Wishes the kids were here to see. He fishes a business card out of his pocket and hands it to Erskine.

"I'd like you to call me if there's anything you think I should know," he says, and then, pointedly: "Anything at all."

Erskine gives a little nod and turns away, picking the items out of the wheelbarrow and stuffing them in his pocket. McAvoy swings a leg over the back of the quad and holds onto the hard plastic at the rear of the padded seat.

"Your coat will get filthy," says Prince.

"Part of the job," says McAvoy.

Prince turns the throttle and performs a smooth U-turn in the courtyard then guns the bike past the nearest outbuilding and onto a road that is almost swamp-like. McAvoy holds on tight and feels the mud spatter against his trouser legs as they head past a row of trees; their branches bare and stark, as if they have been drawn against the purple sky with a stick of charcoal.

After only a minute on the quad, a small outbuilding comes into view. From the front, it is the basic shape of an open envelope. As Prince pulls up outside, McAvoy can see that the roof and the cement between the bricks are in poor repair. The door has a new padlock on it but the wood is so old it bows at the top and the bottom. A slim man could almost slip through the gap.

Prince climbs from the quad and pulls a large bunch of keys from his pocket. He walks to the door and as he starts fumbling with the lock, McAvoy looks around him. They are half a mile from the house. At the rear of the building, the trees give way to an old privet hedge, marking a boundary line long since forgotten. The muddy track beneath his feet continues on, out towards what he takes, in this light, to be a row of greenhouses.

"What's further on?" asks McAvoy, getting his phone from his pocket and pulling up the satellite image. It shows another row of structures and what looks like a prisoner of war camp made of glass. He notes, as he puts his phone away, that he has a perfectly good signal.

"Nurseries," says Prince, opening the door and pocketing the padlock. "Glasshouses. Bloody boiling in the summer. That's where he was working the day of the accident. Like I say, sweaty doesn't cover it. The lads would take it in turns to go and cool down. I won't lie to you, we sometimes gave them a few beers and stuff. I know they were convicts and there are rules but they were good workers and after a bit you start just thinking of them as blokes, y'know? You don't even want to hear their names because once you've got that, you start Googling to try and find stuff out. Only hard bit was keeping order. The regular staff all had mobiles and there were a few cross words when they refused to let the prisoners use them. Saw one little scrawny fella go for one of our leading hands with a cucumber in one hand and a lettuce knife in the other. It's all part of the business, I suppose. Sometimes feels like I'm in a Dickens novel."

McAvoy is standing by the door. It smells damp inside, like wet hay; like the vegetable drawer in a student house.

"No light?"

"No electrics," says Prince.

McAvoy nods and steps inside. He looks at the rotted floor. Above, exposed roof beams stick out from the pitch dark shadows like the ribs of long-sunk ships. He wonders whether one of the lighter patches on the mottled floor represents the spot where the auger used to stand.

"Here," says Prince, nodding at the floor. "Poor lad was skewered. I'll never forget it. Owen was holding his hand but he was already gone."

"Owen?" asks McAvoy, squatting down and moving the wooden planks away. "Thought you didn't want to know names."

"He introduced himself," shrugs Prince. "You don't get many prisoners with good manners. He and Will both shook my hand the first day they came here. Said thanks for the opportunity. Owen was standing behind Will, making sure he didn't let himself down. It was like watching a kid with their dad."

McAvoy presses his hand to the damp ground. A young man died here. His blood soaked into the soft earth. He cannot help wondering if it sits there among the strata of different rocks; a layer of gore among the ancient stone.

"Did the prisoners ever try and get the other workers to bring them things they could take back inside?" asks McAvoy, standing up and sweeping the light from his phone around the bare walls. Old, rusted bits of machinery gather in the corners like metal skeletons.

"Every bloody day," says Prince. "We tried to police it but it's hard on a site this big. We couldn't be blamed if some of our casual workers brought them the odd bit of weed or a pay-as-you-go phone, or whatever. People look for an angle."

"And Will? Did he ever try and persuade anybody to bring him something?"

In the light of the phone, Prince's face is all hollows and shadows but McAvoy can see that he is working out the merits of truth over deceit. He nods.

"Lad was into herbal stuff. He was good at it. Knew what all the herbs were meant for. I had a terrible kidney infection last summer and he told me what to take. Said he'd make it for me if I brought him the stuff."

"And did you?"

"It was only a bit of cumin and parsley and a bit of vegetable glycerine, though that were a bugger to find. Seemed to work too. He brewed it up in my Thermos while he was on his break. Tasted bloody horrible. Lads called him 'Witchy' but he seemed to like that."

McAvoy digests this. Swings his torch around once more and forces himself to do what he must. He squats down and lifts the floorboards. It takes an effort of will to keep his movements nonchalant when he sees the ugly trench beneath. He stands. Breathes out. Kicks at a stone by his feet. He is about to switch the light off and return to the open air when he sees the scratches on the inside of the door. Dozens of names have been scored into the old wood. He crosses over and considers them. Wonders how many different farmhands have sat in the cool gloom of this place and eaten their lunch and drunk their ale and left their mark. He looks for Owen's name first. Fails to find it among the overlapping, misspelled chaos of graffiti. He sees two initials and a date. FW, 43. Finds himself strangely emotional at the thought of touching a carving left there seventy years before. So many names. *Lewis. Gaz. Nigel T. Bam. GED 91. Danny East. HKR. Fuck United.* He traces the words with his finger. Follows them upwards with the light of the torch. Beside the top hinges is something oddly familiar. He would not be able to say if it puts him in mind of Hebrew or Arabic or something else from a textbook, but it is a group of curls and twisted letters; somehow more intricate and expertly placed than the sea of jumbled letters amid which it sits. McAvoy steps back and switches the function on his phone. His eyes fill with white light as he takes a picture of the letters and then the remainder of the door. He turns and takes several more of the rest of the barn, managing to capture Prince in profile in one of the shots. He snaps at random, trying to look as if he knows what he is doing. After a few moments he thanks Prince for his time and returns to the bike, waiting for the foreman to lock up. McAvoy is surprised to see that he does not bother to reattach the padlock.

"Get what you needed?"

McAvoy's reply is lost to the sound of the throttle and the grind of rubber on wet mud.

He doesn't know the answer to the question. Doesn't know why he is investigating or whether Owen wants him to. All he knows is that the only way the auger could have pushed that deep into the soil is if somebody was holding it by the handles and forcing it through the blood and bones of a screaming William Blaylock.

8

Hessle Foreshore
8.32pm

A yellowy half-moon is being sliced into thirds by the great metal strings of the Humber Bridge. The lunar light thrown upon the black waters of the river look like cage bars.

Set back a little way from the rippling water is a row of houses, painted white. One is covered in scaffold and green mesh. It is dark within. Sad, somehow, like a crying clown.

At the rear of the property, an old-fashioned caravan has been wedged into the tiny garden. Warm light spills out. It is filled with the sound of children giggling; of glasses and crockery clinking together; of soft voices and quiet lullabies. It is a cosy space, all floral curtains and laminate floor, built-in wardrobes and an L-shaped sofa. The only jarring note is the slow slurp-slurp-slurp of Trish Pharaoh trying to get the last of the meat off a chicken.

"This is amazing," says Pharaoh, gesturing at the leg she holds in her left hand like a conductor's baton. "Seriously, if this chicken had known what you were going to do it, it would have danced on its ways to the gallows."

Roisin turns from the sink, suds dripping from her polished fingertips all the way down her tanned arms. She smiles, pleased at the compliment.

"My head is now completely full of the idea of a chicken being hanged," she says, the Irish lilt to her voice rich around the sibilant 's'. "I can see its family crying and there's an awful moment when they open the trapdoor."

Pharaoh takes another bite and makes the kind of noise that Roisin normally reserves for foreplay. "Don't care," she says. "If you told me that you'd cook it like this, I'd gladly kick a chicken to death."

Roisin starts laughing and turns back to the washing up. She finished her own meal a couple of hours ago but has got into the habit of making Pharaoh a plate in case she suddenly turns up and starts making noises that suggest she is peckish. On the evenings when she doesn't turn up, Aector is happy to eat two dinners.

"I'm still waiting," sings Pharaoh into the mobile phone she holds at her ear. "Oh bloody hell, Ben, just phone me back."

She terminates the call and huffs a strand of loose hair out of her eyes. Roisin can feel her eyes upon her back. She's pleased she's looking good. It's a little after 8.30 p.m. and she was tempted to change into her night clothes and dressing gown as soon as Aector got home, but both kids had been excitable and Roisin hadn't had time to change. Pharaoh has been here for over an hour now and Roisin thinks it would be impolite or somehow suggestive if she went and slipped into her baseball shirt, loose shorts and leopard-print dressing gown. She's happy as she is, in her velour jogging suit and vest, hooped earrings and hair piled up on top of her head in a loose beehive.

Roisin has stopped remarking upon the irony that she and her family are living in a caravan. Roisin is a traveller and until she was seventeen such places were home. For the past eight years she has lived with Aector, first in his comfortable apartment and then a nice two-bedroomed semi-detached house on the Kingswood estate. Last year she moved into her dream home on Hessle Foreshore. It was partially destroyed in the bomb blast that robbed Roisin of her best friend. While the building is made structurally sound, she and the family are living in a caravan in the back garden. She's quite enjoying being back in familiar surround-ings and the kids are treating every day like a holiday. Only Aector is struggling. He keeps apologising for their situation. Neither Aector nor Roisin are convinced they want to move back into the house when the work is done. It feels tainted, somehow, as though somebody has drawn a great black line through their dreams.

"What's he telling them in there, War and Peace?"

For the past half an hour, Aector has been telling Fin and Lilah their bedtime story. It's a long-running saga involving imps, goblins, spaceships and an elephant on roller skates. It started out as a Scottish folk tale he remembered from his youth but Fin had interfered like the worst kind of Hollywood producer and he's had to make accommodations.

"He's supposed to be settling them down," says Roisin, smil-ing. "By the time I get in there Lilah will be bouncing off the walls."

As if on cue, there is a great trill of laughter from behind the flimsy bedroom door. Roisin angles herself away from Pharaoh to hide the look of pure delight that crosses her face.

"Snoring like walruses," says Aector, ducking under the doorframe.

"We're not," comes the response from the bedroom, followed by more giggles.

Roisin shakes her head at him. "You're an eejit," she says.

He bends down to kiss her cheek. As he straightens up, he bangs his head on the ceiling light and gives the sigh of a man who has reconciled himself to spending the rest of his life saying "ouch".

"You're nothing but lumps and bruises," says Pharaoh, putting the chicken leg back on the plate and wearing the face of somebody far from happy about the continued absence of rosemary-and-thyme roast potatoes.

"You should see him with his shirt off," says Roisin, with a little glance at Aector. He colours at once.

McAvoy crosses the small living area and manages to fold himself in at the round kitchen table. It is covered in loose sheets of paper, scribbled notes, photographs and official reports.

"Any joy with Ben?" asks McAvoy.

"Bloody system's down again," says Pharaoh, taking a black cigarette from the case in her handbag and lighting up. She catches McAvoy's disapproving glare and sticks out her tongue. "Five a day, man. I'm down to five. And don't go on about going outside. This is a caravan. We are outside."

Roisin brings her an ashtray, wiping her hands on a fluffy cream towel. She exposes dainty fingers, rich with gold, silver and platinum; bangles on her wrists and tiger-stripes on her fingernails.

"You said there was nail polish in the wheelbarrow," says Pharaoh, her memory jogged. "What was the other stuff?"

"Looked like anti-bac."

"And they said they'd been cleaning out the Ponderosa?"

"Aye. They were flustered. Looked like they wished they hadn't spoken."

Pharaoh breathes out smoke and looks at her phone. Her favourite Detective Constable, Ben Neilsen, is currently working his magic on the various databases the Serious and Organised Unit has access to. As ever, the system is playing up and Pharaoh's patience is fraying. She picks up the photo of William Blaylock's corpse skewered to the floor in the outbuilding. She tuts.

"How can anybody look at that and say it was an accident?"

"Health and Safety said it wasn't impossible."

"But 'not impossible' doesn't mean likely."

"It was good enough for the coroner."

"It's not good enough for me."

"His arms," says McAvoy. "That's what Owen said."

Pharaoh peers at the picture. Puts it down and rummages through her paperwork until she finds the post-mortem report.

She skims through the descriptions of his injuries and starts reading aloud.

"...extensive tattoos on his forearms and across his chest."

McAvoy picks up the discarded photo. He squints. Retrieves his reading glasses from his shirt pocket and puts them on. Shakes his head.

"Roisin, your eyes are better than mine, can you make this out?"

Pharaoh grins across the table, seeming to enjoy the naughtiness of letting a civilian view the paperwork. She would be hypocritical to criticise. She allows her eldest daughter to type up her reports in exchange for exemption from tidying.

Roisin peers at the photo, untroubled by the injuries to Blaylock's torso. Focuses, as asked, on the ink on William's arms. She glances at McAvoy, puzzled.

"Is this a test?" she asks, half-serious. "You're not making fun?"

McAvoy looks a little hurt. "I never make fun."

Roisin picks up a pen and a loose sheet of paper from the table-top. She doodles a quick symbol and shows it to McAvoy. He considers it for a moment and then sits back in his chair. He takes the pen and sketches another symbol.

"That's an 'O'," says Roisin.

McAvoy smiles. "Owen was wearing that as a pendant. Looked like it had been made from a paper clip. Show me more."

Roisin grins, clearly pleased to be involved, and draws a longer symbol. It looks like a succession of swirls with tails; like a language made up of the number '9'.

"That's my name," she says. "Do you want me to do yours?"

McAvoy is scrolling through his phone. He shows the screen to Roisin, who squints and starts copying it down.

"Would you like to fill me in?" asks Pharaoh, sitting forward and feeling a little left out.

"This is the Wiccan alphabet," says Roisin, sticking her tongue out in concentration as she turns the crude scratches from the back of the wooden door into something elegant and strangely other-worldly. "He's got it on his left arm, see. Those letters you can see in the picture, they're m, n, o, p and q. Give me a second, I'll work out what the graffiti says. I haven't looked at this stuff in years. My Mam would be better."

McAvoy and Pharaoh exchange a look. Pharaoh shrugs.

"This was scrawled on the door of the barn where William died," says McAvoy, putting his hands behind his head and thumping his knuckles on the beige wall. "I only photographed it because it seemed familiar."

"Oh, this was on a door, was it? Any lemongrass?" asks Roisin, brightly.

McAvoy laughs excitedly. He looks startled. "There was an incident at the prison," he says. "Owen took the blame when William nabbed some spices from the kitchen. Lemongrass. Dill. He mentioned another one. Salt, pepper and vinegar."

"Sounds like a skipping chant," mutters Pharaoh.

"Salt, pepper and vinegar as a paste," says Roisin, still drawing. "You rub it on doors and windows and it protects you from people who want to harm you."

Pharaoh makes a face. "Does it?"

Roisin shrugs. "It's a very basic spell. Not even a spell, to be honest. More like a superstition. The lemongrass is more interesting. If you want to make somebody fall in love with you, you write their name or take a picture of them and wrap it in three twists of lemongrass. It's the sort of thing teenage girls do when they buy a Wiccan book. It's quite sweet."

Pharaoh knows she looks as though somebody has just cracked an egg down the back of her blouse. "How do you know this stuff?"

"It's not a big leap from making poultices and ointments and putting the right herbs in a chicken dinner to knowing which plants and flowers have different powers. And when you're a teenager and don't know much about the world, doing a spell makes as much sense as praying, though you'd never say that out loud. I did the lemongrass charm myself when I was about 13. Wrote the name of this big, burly copper on it. Still got it somewhere ..."

McAvoy blushes instantly.

"We know Will was into this stuff," he says, after clearing

his throat. "He made stuff for other prisoners. Read their alternative horoscopes. I wonder how it helps."

Roisin finishes her drawing and is about to speak when Pharaoh's phone rings. It's a call from Ben Neilsen's personal mobile phone and the ringtone is Sexy Back by Justin Timberlake. Her ringtone for McAvoy used to be set to I Would Walk 500 Miles by The Proclaimers but she had to change it to a basic ring when it went off during a post mortem and reduced the pathologist to fits of giggles.

"Ben, my sweet. Tell me what you've got for me."

Roisin and McAvoy look at one another while Pharaoh talks. He is glowing with pride and she is beaming in return.

"Ben, you are a bloody diamond. Keep your phone on. And your trousers. See you later."

Pharaoh hangs up, pleased. She's been writing on the first piece of paper she could find and winces a little as she realises it's a report into Blaylock's injuries.

"It says here he had soft palette damage," she says, distracted. "A cut to the roof of his mouth. Any ideas?"

McAvoy shakes his head. Nods at the phone, as if to encourage her to fill him in.

"The car you saw at the farm is registered to an Alison Gresswell. DOB 23.07.79. Lives on Plimsoll Way. That's Victoria Dock. Three points on her licence and..." she beats her hands on the table, theatrically... "received a suspended sentence in 2011 for perjury. She provided a false alibi for her partner, Michael Bee, as in Bumble. Hang on a second..." She turns the phone around to show a mugshot of a man with a tattoo of a demon on his neck. "This your friend?"

McAvoy nods, looking at the doodle Roisin has created on the page.

"We've run Erskine and Prince through the PNC. Both squeaky clean, though Erskine is behind on his VAT payments. Ben has gone through Blaylock's personal prison file. Only visitors he ever got were his mum and an uncle. He lost privileges along with a dozen other inmates when they were found in the greenhouses at Bull Sands with a mobile phone. The phone was seized. Ben's put in a request for the SIM card to be couri-

ered over from the evidence store. Apparently it's with
Lincolnshire Police. What else? Your friend, Michael Bee. He's
done two stretches, one for armed robbery. Last did a year in
Lincoln, released in 2012. Was monitored by Probation Services
for 12 months upon release and they were satisfied. He had a
job at a certain Shepton Farm at Gilberdyke. I think it's fair to
say he doesn't work there any more."

"His last jail stretch," says McAvoy, sitting forward. "Can we
get his file?"

"Not without this getting a lot more serious," says Pharaoh.
"We'd need the permission of the Governor, and that might do
more than ruffle some feathers."

McAvoy looks at his boss, clearly expecting more. Pharaoh
smiles and lights another of her black cigarettes.

"His last stretch," she says, easing out a plume of smoke.
"Wounding. He glassed a bloke in the Bay Horse down
Wincolmlee. Case was straightforward enough. He was acting
as a driver for a working girl. Punter roughed her up. He found
the punter and gave him a hiding. He started off saying he
wasn't even there, that he was at home with his partner, Gresswell. She gave a statement backing him up. When he changed
his statement, she was charged alongside him. He did some
time, she got a suspended sentence."

McAvoy realises that a mug of tea has arrived in front of
him. He takes a swig, nodding a smile at Roisin.

"Occupation?"

"Gresswell is registered as a company director of two firms.
Property company and a mobile nail franchise. Handsome
turnover. They're registered at an address in Wincolmlee."

"Handy."

"Yes."

"When it came to court, was there a witness statement from
the working girl to support his mitigation?"

Pharaoh grins, clearly proud of her sergeant. "Ben's pinging
a name over now. She didn't give evidence but she did provide a
statement. The lad's also looking through a list of recent
releases from Bull Sands to see if there are any friendly names
who might talk to us."

Roisin looks between the two of them.

"You know the herbs that Will got in trouble for taking?" she asks, cautiously. "Can you remember exactly what they were?"

McAvoy puts his head back, obviously thinking hard. "Salt, pepper, vinegar, mustard. Lovely Speedwell. He told me to ask my wife."

Roisin nods, smiling. "He wanted to tell you but couldn't be sure who was listening," she says. "Speedwell. You brew it in tea and it helps get rid of your colds."

"And?" asks Pharaoh, as her phone rings.

"Its other name is Veronica."

"And?"

Roisin nods at the swirls on the page. "That's what the dead lad carved in the door there. Owen wanted to steer you but had to put on a show for whoever was watching. He wants your help, Aector. You're doing the right thing."

Pharaoh opens her phone and snorts. "The prostitute in question," she says, shaking her head. "Annabel Veronica Dolan. 24 years old. Last address was in Gipsyville. And Aector, you'll love this, Ben's been through the list of prisoners currently out on temporary licence and cross-referenced them against Michael Bee. He's found a James Kinchie. Right age-range. Served two years of an eight-year sentence for his part in a massive identity fraud. Released to an address in Goole. It was a big deal for SOCA."

"SOCA?" asks Roisin.

"Serious and Organised Crime Agency. It's only been a few years and I still can't get used to the name change. National Crime Agency now, but ask them and they'll tell you they're Britain's answer to the FBI. Big boys. Wankers, largely, but they owe us a favour."

McAvoy looks at the name on the pad. Squints a little.

"If William carved her name, or wrote it and wrapped it in lemongrass, he wanted her to love him," says Roisin, quietly. "I wonder how they knew each other."

Pharaoh starts keying letters into the search engine on her phone. After a moment she slides it across the table to McAvoy.

"Angels," he reads. "Escort agency."

"Third girl from the left," says Pharaoh. "I know my eyes are older than Roisin's, but that looks suspiciously like a tattoo of the Tree of Life on her thigh. That's vaguely witchy and wiccan, isn't it?"

"Ronnie Payne," he reads. "Looks the right sort of age. You think?"

Pharaoh nods. "Worth a shot."

"You think this is the girl?" Roisin asks. "You're going to ask her about Will?"

McAvoy says nothing. His cheeks are starting to colour. Roisin puts her hand upon his, stroking his scars with her thumb.

"Don't worry, I'll be there to hold his hand," says Pharaoh, reaching across and taking a sip of his tea. "After all, it says she does couples."

9

I t wasn't a conscious decision, but Pharaoh put on a distinctly more eye-catching set of clothes when she got up this morning. She always looks good, with her ever-present biker boots, leather jacket and large sunglasses, but they tend to be accessories for a plain black dress, or black trousers and a V-neck jumper. Today, she dipped into the back of the wardrobe for something that would make her feel a little better about herself in the company of a woman who men pay for sex. She has been self-conscious about her appearance for the past couple of years, having gained a little weight on her diet of wine, re-heated pasta and cigarettes. Despite being a strong, intelligent and successful woman, there are days when she would give it all up just to be thin. Today is one of those days.

She looks at herself in the bathroom mirror. She's wearing a white blouse, fitted black jacket and a knee-length camel skirt that clings to her hips and thighs. She's still wearing her biker boots, but her nylons have a line up the back. She caught McAvoy looking as they got out of the car. She was so pleased that she even forgot to tease him about it.

Pharaoh checks her make-up. Even with it, she looks tired. Feels it too. Feels old and fat and bloody ridiculous.

"Mutton," she hisses at her reflection. Then, as she remembers the silly smile on her face as McAvoy admired her, she adds: "Stupid bitch."

She says it louder than she means to. Clamps a hand over her mouth in case she spews any more self-loathing. Forces herself to focus.

She is standing in the bathroom of Flat 6, Oberon House. It belongs to DC Ben Neilsen and sits in the heart of what used to be Hull's Fruit Market. Millions of pounds in regeneration money have been spent on this area. It's a prime location, overlooking the Marina and its bobbing yachts and the elegant pathways that lead down to The Deep aquarium on Sammy's Point. The Oberon used to be a pub and has been sympathetically converted into the closest thing Hull can boast to a block of luxury apartments. Given Ben's reputation for bedroom gymnastics, Pharaoh felt it an appropriate place to arrange the meeting with Veronica. Ben didn't argue, wilting in the face of Pharaoh's implacable gaze and half smile. He agreed to let her and McAvoy use the flat on the proviso that nobody looked in the drawers under his bed.

Veronica has been here for ten minutes now and Pharaoh is starting to worry about what is going on in the living room. Standing at the front window, she and McAvoy watched Veronica arrive. She was five minutes early for their 11am appointment. She sat and waited in her Vauxhall Corsa, applying a second coat of lipstick while McAvoy and Pharaoh hid behind the curtains like nosy neighbours and waited for her to ring the bell. When she emerged from the car, she looked more like her voice than her photograph. It was Pharaoh who made the date, calling Ronnie through the website and explaining that it was her husband's fantasy to have a threesome with a stranger. Ronnie explained what she was willing to do and what she was not. As it turned out, the only things she wasn't willing to do were things that Pharaoh had never heard of. When Pharaoh mentioned that her husband had a kinky side, Ronnie laughed and said that she'd never met a man who didn't. They agreed a time, a place and a price.

The woman who got out of the car had probably been a

looker when she was a teenager. Five years on, what shine she had has been squeezed out of her. The woman who sits on the sofa with McAvoy is thin as a nail. She has shoulder-length brown hair and she has accentuated her already prominent cheekbones with smears of red, so that it looks as though she has been struck across both cheeks with a cane. She arrived wearing a long coat over a short black dress, stockings and shoes that were clearly too big for size three feet.. Pharaoh slipped into the bathroom as she arrived, stepping into the bathtub and pulling the shower curtain closed. For a brief spell a decade ago, Pharaoh worked in the vice unit and has run several operations like this. She has never known a working girl get straight down to business. In her experience, they excuse themselves and head for the bathroom, where they place a phone call to a colleague or a driver and let them know where they are. Then they look at themselves in the mirror. They get ready like an actor applying make-up and wig. And then they go and let strangers into themselves for money. Veronica was no different. She made a quick call on an expensive iPhone and told her contact that she was at the address. The client was a big man. Good-looking, if a little battered around the edges. She said that the woman was running late but the man had paid for an hour up front. Everything was fine. As she hung up she opened the medicine cupboard and looked at a few bottles. Behind the shower curtain, Pharaoh allowed herself a tiny smile for remembering to put a few female items in there. Veronica didn't look in the mirror as she left the room. She gave herself a spray of perfume, put her gum in the toilet and flushed the chain. Then she tottered out on her too-big heels.

Here, now, Pharaoh listens on her mobile to the conversation in the next room. She can tell that McAvoy is running out of excuses and decides to let him squirm for another minute or two before emerging from the bathroom. His mobile phone sits in the pocket of his suit jacket, casually thrown over the arm of the chair. Pharaoh can hear every word. She told him not to seem too nice, to be like an average punter and to keep the conversation friendly but with a hint of sexiness to it. McAvoy looked at her as if she'd told him to slip into suspenders and nipple clamps. He's just being himself. She can picture him, red-faced and looking at the floor, hands folded in his lap in case anybody throws themselves at him. At times like these, Pharaoh wonders how the hell he ever got together with Roisin.

"She won't be long," comes Aector's voice. He has said this fourteen times already.

"She's an understanding woman," says Ronnie. "Not many wives buy women for their men."

"No?"

"Well, a few. But there are often complications."

"What do you mean?"

"Y'know, they think they're up for it but the second something starts to happen they get jealous. It's like men in threesomes."

"I'm sorry?"

"It's sexy when you're aroused. You like the idea of another man having a go with your wife or girlfriend. But the second it's over you feel like killing them."

"I suppose."

"You look nervous. Are you okay?"

"I've never really done anything like this."

"Would you like a massage? Relax you?"

"No, I'm fine..."

"I've got poppers. They take the edge off."

"Not really my thing. Sorry."

"Are you sure you want to do this? It's no problem. I don't want to force you. Is this your fantasy or your wife's?"

"Both. Hers. I don't know."

Listening in, Pharaoh frowns. She wants him to tell the story the way they planned. Wants him to bait the hook.

"I was inside, y'see," says McAvoy, quietly.

"Inside?"

"Prison."

"Yeah? You don't seem the sort."

"Tax fraud."

"Ah. Soft time, then."

"Mostly. Did my last two months at Bull Sands?"

"Yeah?"

"Yeah. Mate of mine recommended you. Talked about you a lot, in fact."

"Yeah?"

"Yeah. Sad case, it was. Got himself hurt."

"Yeah?"

Pharaoh sighs into the phone, urging him to get on with it.

"Will," says McAvoy. "Will Blaylock."

"Don't think I know that name. Sorry. Anyway, shall we get on?"

"Not without my wife. You sure you don't know Will?"

"I said so."

"He was really specific. Ronnie, that was what he said. Told me to look you up when I got out. Said you were the best."

"That's kind, but like I said, I don't know the name."

"Do you have anything else beside poppers? Coke, maybe?"

"No, that's illegal."

"Will said you might be able to hook me up."

"I don't know Will. I said so. And I'm a busy gir,l so if we're not going to do this then I'd better be off."

"I've paid for an hour."

"I don't care. I'm going."

"Please don't. I'm sorry, I didn't mean to offend you. Hey, you're trembling. Don't be scared."

"Please let me go. I've not said anything. I won't say anything. Please."

"Ronnie, you're shaking. Come here, it's okay... Christ, my eyes!!"

Pharaoh yanks open the bathroom door and runs into the living room just as Ronnie comes charging out of it. Pharaoh reacts fastest and grabs the scrawny woman by her wrist, forcing it up and spinning her around back into the living room. McAvoy has the heels of both hands pressed to his eyes and tears streaming down his red cheeks. He's hissing in pain.

Pharaoh looks at the floor and sees the vial of pepper-spray. She pushes Ronnie forward onto the black leather sofa. She shuffles backwards on her bottom; her dress riding up and stockings coming unclipped as she wraps her arms around her head to ward off a blow.

"I'm sorry, I'm sorry, I never said, I never said..."

"Stay there," orders Pharaoh, and crosses to McAvoy. She pulls his hands away from his face and looks up into his red, teary eyes. She winces.

"Go wash them out," she says. "Bit of salt in a shot-glass. Warm water. Put it over your eye and open your eyelid. Blink a few times. You'll be good as new."

McAvoy scrunches his eyes up again, growling at the pain. He looks like a hugely inflated toddler trying to be brave. As he leaves the room he knocks over a lamp and apologises to the air as he bumbles down the corridor.

Pharaoh turns back to Ronnie. She has pulled her legs up and the tattoo of the Green Man is clearly visible on her thigh. So, too, are the enlarged blue veins of a serial user.

"Smile for me," says Pharaoh, flatly.

"I'm sorry," stammers Ronnie.

"You heard. Show me your teeth."

"I don't understand."

"You don't need to. Smile."

Trembling, Ronnie shows her teeth. They are the colour of toffees, and one incisor has split in two.

"What you on? Miaow-miaow?"

Crying now, Ronnie nods. "I'm clean of the smack."

"Good for you. Your mother must be proud."

Pharaoh looks at her. She's a pathetic specimen, exuding fear from every pore. Pharaoh knows already the life that she has lived. Some street workers develop a hardness that keeps everybody else at a distance, while others are desperate for affection and fall in love with anybody who shows them kindness. Their hearts never toughen. Pharaoh can see at once what kind of person Ronnie is.

"Will Blaylock," says Pharaoh. "The truth."

"I haven't said a word!" shouts Ronnie, and her voice cracks. A bubble of snot blows out her nose and she wipes it away with her bare wrist.

"No, you haven't," says Pharaoh. "But you're going to."

"I won't. I swear I won't."

Pharaoh sucks her lower lip, thinking. Then she chuckles. "Can I ask, Ronnie – who do you think we are?"

"You work for them. You're trying to scare me. And you have. I swear, I won't say anything!"

Ronnie's handbag is at the far end of the sofa. Pharaoh crosses to it and picks it up. Inside are sex toys, restraints, lubricants, lipsticks, gels and nail varnish. She rakes through, pulls out a packet of tissues and hands one to Ronnie, who takes it with a shaking hand.

Pharaoh goes to the large front window and looks out at the city. The roofs of two old fruit warehouses spoil the view across the Old Town but she can still make out Holy Trinity Church and the head of the golden statue outside the Magistrate's Court. On Castle Street, the traffic is gridlocked and the rain swirling around the cars and buildings is falling at the rate that leaves drivers unsure whether to put their wipers on intermittent or constant.

"I've got a surprise for you," says Pharaoh, turning her back on the city and enjoying the elegant neatness of Neilsen's apartment. She has found little to make fun of him about, save the loud floral wallpaper in his bedroom and the school photos in the drawer under his bed.

Veronica looks up, all folded in on herself. She seems braced for violence.

"My name is Detective Superintendent Patricia Pharaoh," Pharaoh says, sweetly. "That chap in the bathroom is Detective Sergeant McAvoy. You can call him Hector, if you like, though you will call me Detective Superintendent. You've just pepper-sprayed him. You've just told me that you think I'm here to frighten you into silence. You look like you're about to jump out of the window. All of this leads me to surmise that you have something to tell me that I am going to find jolly interesting. So, let me ask again – does the name William Blaylock mean anything to you?"

Ronnie's eyes have grown steadily wider and now tears spill, carving lines in her rouged cheeks. As she wipes her eyes, one of her false lashes comes off and is left stuck to the side of her head like a half-eaten centipede.

"I don't know him," she says. "I don't."

Pharaoh sighs. She holds up her hand and shows Ronnie that she has taken her phone from her bag.

"It's going to be about 45 minutes until you have to check in and tell whoever it is that looks after you that you've finished. We've got a nice quiet place and lots of time. You're safe and warm and I can promise you nobody is going to ask you to touch yourself or take your top off or stick anything in your mouth other than a cup of tea and a biscuit. This could be the best part of your day."

"I can't," says Ronnie, and she sucks on her wrist with a childishness that makes Pharaoh want to hold her. "They'll kill me."

Pharaoh considers her. Then she slips out of her leather jacket and puts it around Ronnie's shoulders. She removes two black cigarette from her pocket and lights them both. Wordlessly, she places one between Ronnie's lips. They smoke in silence. At length, Ronnie waves in the direction of the bathroom.

"I'm sorry about your friend. He didn't seem like a punter."

"He doesn't seem much like a human."

"I didn't mean to spray him. I thought he was working for them. He's massive."

"He's a massive idiot."

"I do want to help you. I just can't."

"I want you to help me. And I think you can."

McAvoy comes back into the living room. His eyes are still red and the front of his shirt is soaking. He sees the two women smoking and goes into the kitchen. He returns with two saucers and places one on each end of the sofa, as if he is feeding cats. Then he goes to the recliner and sits, blinking hard.

"You look like you've got wind," says Pharaoh.

"I'm sorry," says Ronnie. "I thought you were trying to hurt me."

"I wouldn't do that," says McAvoy, making fists with his hands so as not to scratch at his eyes. "We want to help you."

"Aren't we all a fucking helpful bunch," says Pharaoh,

knocking the end of her cigarette into the ashtray. "Now, can we stop fucking about and get some answers, please?"

"I can't," says Ronnie, crossing her legs and squeezing her arms into her sides.

"We've been through that," says Pharaoh, dismissively. "Thing is, I'm sure your phone has all sorts of exciting messages in it and it wouldn't take a moment to unearth them all. We could walk you out of here in handcuffs for assaulting an officer and we could time it so that whoever looks after you is sitting outside at the perfect moment. We could laugh and joke and make it seem like we're all best friends and you've helped us out. We could do all sorts of things to fuck life up for you, Ronnie. But we don't want to do that. We want to find out who killed Will Blaylock. If you give us enough help we could even register you as an informant and get you some money. You have so many more options than you think you do. But if you tell me you're not going to help me, then I have no choice but to act like a total cow, and that will cause my sergeant here all sorts of emotional turmoil and then his wife will make some sort of potion to soothe his bile duct and I think that will just about push me over the edge. So spare us all, and tell me about Will."

Ronnie looks up at the mention of potions. She focuses on McAvoy. "Rosewater," she says. "If she has some, bathe your eyes with it. You'll be fine."

Pharaoh throws her hands up. "Am I the only person in Britain who thinks that rosemary is for lamb and lemongrass stops being useful when you've eaten your Thai curry? What is wrong with you people?"

McAvoy sits forward in his chair. He looks at Ronnie with his red-seamed eyes and seems, for a moment, like a poet weeping for the ugliness of the world. If he did such things on purpose, Pharaoh would marvel at his powers of manipulation. Instead, she simply lets him do what he does better than anybody she has ever worked with. He makes people want to help him. He makes them see a different kind of world. She has seen him become father, son, lover and confidante in the eyes of those he opens up to, has seen battle-hardened villains break down and confess rather than see any more disappointment in those liquid brown eyes.

"Can I tell you what I think?" asks McAvoy, in the voice he uses to calm his children and shush horses. "Is it Veronica, by the way? What do your friends call you?"

"It's Annabel. Anna, really."

"Anna, that's lovely. Anna, I know that right now you're scared and confused and you're trying to work out the right thing to do. I have no doubt that some very nasty people have made you feel scared. I hate the thought of that. I want you to feel safe and appreciated and all the things that it's everybody's right to wake up feeling every day. And to do that, I have to lock up those bad men. That probably sounds terrifying. Your head is probably full of images of having to go into police stations and courtrooms and going into hiding for months until a trial comes up. Well, I can't promise you that I won't ask you, some way down the line, to give evidence formally but here, today, I'm not asking for that. I'm asking you for a little help. I don't really need you to do much more than nod, and perhaps mutter a couple of names. Then you can clean yourself up and leave here on time and go about your day knowing that, at the very least, things won't get any worse for you than they have been, and that they will quite possibly get better."

Ronnie manages a little smile. She sniffs and looks ashamed at making such a crude noise in front of McAvoy.

"I've got a bit of a theory, you see," says McAvoy, leaning back in his chair and twitching his mouth into a grin that his new best friend is unable to resist mimicking. "You were right when you asked about the whole herbalism thing. My wife is wonderful at it. And she told me what it means when you bind a lover's name in lemongrass. She told me about the Wiccan alphabet. What it all adds up to is a young man who was very much infatuated with a young woman by the name of 'Ronnie'. Now, I'm making quite a few leaps of intuition here and can't be sure of anything without your help, but I've had the word 'Ponderosa' running around in my head all night. I've been thinking about a pot of nail varnish and some anti-bac in a wheelbarrow out at Shepton Farm. I've been thinking about a brothel madam and her husband and how much money could be made providing services for prisoners. And the picture I have in my head is a cruel one and it makes me angry and sad, but more than anybody else, it makes me angry and sad for you."

Ronnie squeezes her face up. Fresh tears spill.

"It's over now," she says. "I don't want to be part of it. I never did."

McAvoy nods. Were he able to reach, he would be patting her hand.

"Michael Bee," he says. "He got a job at Shepton Farm and persuaded the owner to let him use one of the outbuildings as a brothel for the prisoners on day release. No doubt the casual workers too. He paid the farmer a cut and he used the girls his wife was running."

Ronnie nods, sniffing into her hand.

"One of those clients was William Blaylock. He saw your tattoo. Maybe he even talked to you about the things he was interested in. He fell for you."

"He didn't deserve what happened," mutters Ronnie. She looks across to Pharaoh, who is already lighting her another cigarette. She takes it gratefully.

"I think Will got upset at the idea of other prisoners spending time with you. Perhaps he made a fuss. Perhaps he threatened to have the thing shut down. And for that, he got himself killed in a way that would send a warning to anybody who even thought about stepping out of line."

"He thought he was in love with me," says Ronnie, pushing her hair back and exposing the cheap hair extensions that grip her own short, dark locks.

"When did it start?"

"It was already running when Mike Bee contacted me. Said there was easy money. Regular punters. Quick work."

"And The Ponderosa?"

"It's like a lodge, out at the back of the farm. Looks a bit like a Wild West ranch in miniature. It's named after some cowboy show, I think. Erskine had it built for holiday lets but never got it finished. Mike did it up for us. There were three girls, taking turns. I started last April."

"And Will was a client?"

"Sort of."

"How so?"

"Do you know about the phoneline? The videos?"

Pharaoh jumps in before McAvoy can answer. "Yes. We do."

"He was spending everything he had to be able to talk to me. Even before he was eligible for day-release he saw me on the webcam. He saw my tattoos. Showed me his. We got talking. He said he was in love with me before we even met."

"And when he did get day-release?"

"He was too nervous at first. Paid for his turn but we just talked. He was nice."

"And how did he feel about you sleeping with other prisoners?"

"We didn't talk about that. He just kept saying he loved me and that when he got out we could start a life together. I've heard that so many times."

"The video streaming," says Pharaoh. "That was Bee's friend, yes? Kinchie."

"I just know him as Jimmy. He was inside with Mike. They saw an opportunity. They had us girls doing live shows for prisoners. They'd pay to be in the audience, all crowded around a mobile phone. They could tell us what they wanted to see. What they wanted to do. The money went to Mike and we took our cut."

McAvoy scratches at his beard. "When I went to the farm yesterday, Bee was threatening Erskine."

"One of his girls told me that Mike was furious. Erskine shut things down. He cleaned out The Ponderosa."

"Why?"

"When Will died it was too risky to carry on streaming the videos or sorting dates with the prisoners. But Mike started things up again not so long back. Different market," says Ronnie, looking away and letting out a breath that trembles. "Different prisoners. Mike's not letting Erskine say no, but Erskine's standing his ground. He's scared of somebody more terrifying than Mike, though don't ask me who because I don't know. Mike's been asking more money than ever. He always says there's money in people with specialist tastes and prison provides a hell of a lot of customers."

McAvoy's gaze darkens. A stillness comes over him and his voice is suddenly cold as a marble headstone.

"Kids?"

"I'm not involved anymore. I just do calls. People's houses."

"Who is it you're scared of, Anna?" asks Pharaoh. "Who did you think we were?"

"After Will died, Mike told me they didn't need me at The Ponderosa any more. He told me to keep my mouth shut. I didn't hear much from him for a bit and then a couple of months back he came to my house. Told me that whatever I heard, there was nothing happening at The Ponderosa. It was over. And if anybody asked that was what I was to say. I didn't know why he was so wound up but he has a hell of a temper and I said he could trust me."

"Do you think he was scared of somebody?"

Ronnie bites at her wrist again. "He's not easily scared. He's massive and he doesn't let people tell him what to do. He was so angry about Will dying out at the farm. Said it interrupted business, that it could have been done somewhere else. But then he was all smiles and had money in his pocket, acting like the big man again. The next thing he was in my face and threatening me. I don't know what happened. I would never have told you any of this if you hadn't made me."

McAvoy nods, as if accepting the accusation. He turns his attention to Pharaoh, who is still digesting the word 'kids' and feeling as if she would like to be sick and then drown a paedophile in it.

"I don't understand this," he says to her. "What's going on at the farm is horrific but why kill Will? If Bee was that upset about his death then it makes him an unlikely suspect."

Pharaoh holds up her hands as she reads a text. As she does so, McAvoy turns back to Ronnie.

"Did you know an inmate named Owen?" he asks. "Was he a client at the farm?"

"Owen?" asks Ronnie. "That was Will's friend. We never met, no. But Will spoke about him. Admired him like a big brother or something. It was Owen that Will was talking about the last time I saw him. It was the day before he died. He'd said that it would be our first time. He really wanted us to make love. That's what he called it – making love, as if I hadn't just been fucked by half a dozen other blokes. But when he got to the bedroom of the Ponderosa he was shaking. Bleeding from the mouth. He wouldn't tell me what had happened but he said he had to do something he didn't want to. Said he would tell Owen and Owen would help him make it okay. Then he left. Next day Mike told me we had to get out of there because somebody had been killed over at one of the farm buildings. I just knew it was Will. I don't know how I felt about him being alive but I was sad he was dead."

McAvoy is staring at the painting above the fireplace, lost in an image of a young Parisian boy in oversized boots holding a baguette. Pharaoh interrupts his thoughts.

"Ben," she says. "He's worked through the inmate files he can access. A couple of nights before Will was killed, there was an incident in his room. His roommate was attacked in his sleep. He woke up to find somebody sitting on his chest and smashing him in the teeth, knocking most of them out. Left him in a hell of a state. Will was prime suspect but there were no witnesses. The governor ordered an investigation but Will was allowed to keep working at the farm. When the toothless bastard woke up, he said he had no memory of the incident, though I reckon we can safely assume that was bollocks. He just wanted the coast clear to make his own arrangements for revenge."

"Who was the inmate?"

"Elton Flemyng. Nickname of Kremlin. Don't know why. Nasty piece of work who's becoming a force to be reckoned with up in Newcastle. Stepped into the vacuum left by our friend Mr Nock."

McAvoy stares at her, examining her face through a caul of painful memories and weeping wounds.

"There's more. I can see it in your face."

"Elton's brother Tyrone is missing. So are two of his crew."

"Coincidence?"

"Don't be a fucking moron."

McAvoy sits still, blinking so ferociously that he splashes a tear onto the end of his nose.

"You think?" asks McAvoy. "Seriously?"

Pharaoh nods.

Ronnie looks between them, seeking answers. McAvoy turns to her, eyes half-closed.

"Will was given orders to hurt Elton Flemyng. And when he carried them out, he paid with his life." He turns to Pharaoh. "You think Flemyng's still in danger?"

Pharaoh shrugs. "I hope so."

10

The line of yellow light that frames the doorway is not really enough to see by, but Mahon has been in this small, cramped cupboard since before dawn and his amber eyes have grown accustomed to the darkness. He does not need the torch that sits in the pocket of his quilted coat, resting against the handle of the silver meat cleaver. He has spent much of his life in places like this. During his long incarceration he found himself in repeated solitary confinement and enjoyed the nights more than the days. The light always troubled him more. It made a mirror of every surface, each harsh bulb on a painted wall showing him his own ruined face. Better to rule the shadows than bow to the light.

He is comfortable here, in this supply cupboard on the second floor of the Britesmile Centre on Nottingham's leafy West Bridgford estate. His car is two streets away, parked in a gap where CCTV cameras fail to overlap. He broke in at 4 a.m., disabling the alarm with the same practised ease that other men tie their shoes. He switched the system back once inside and then found his hiding place. He has not moved since.

In the surgery down the corridor, a dentist by the name of Dr Malcolm is fitting Elton Flemyng with a second set of veneers. He has undergone three months of expensive dental work at different dental practices but his appointment here today with this expensive consultant will finally give him the smile he seeks. Steel posts have been drilled through his gums and into his jawbone for the eight implants he requires to repair his shattered smile. Once complete, Flemyng will look a lot better than he did when his cellmate Will Blaylock sat on his chest and smashed his teeth in last summer. Mahon has worked hard to bring Blaylock here, to this quiet building. Blaylock's other appointments have been at hospitals and busy surgeries that were ill-suited to Mahon's needs. This final appointment at the dentist's private practice offers much better odds of success. Mahon will not allow himself any moment of self-congratulation. He is doing this because he feels it must be done and because he does not know how else to live his life.

Mahon would admit to this kill being one of the more difficult to arrange. He could have had Elton Flemyng murdered in prison but that would have been riddled with complications. He enjoys being thought of as dead and if somebody were caught having killed Elton at his behest, Mahon knows they would happily roll over and give him up. Moreover, Mahon wants the kill himself. Not for pleasure, but to satisfy his own code. The Flemyngs betrayed Mr Nock, and it is Mahon's job to avenge that slight.

Outside the store cupboard he hears voices. The receptionist and the dental nurse, talking in the corridor. He does not need to check his watch to be certain that the time is right. Flemyng will be in the chair, head back, mouth open. Mahon hopes that the dentist will pose no problem. He does not like hurting innocents.

In the darkness, Mahon thinks back to the last time he stood, immobile; an obsidian statue sunk in black tar. It was last summer, hidden in the shadows of that tacky, ranch-style cabin on the outer reaches of Shepton Farm. He had closed his eyes as the first three men took their turn with the skinny girl. He had no desire to watch their fumblings. Then came the boy, with his tattooed arms and his sweaty forehead. The boy who had fallen for the whore and who shared a cell with Elton. Mahon took him as soon as he pushed open the cabin door. The boy didn't know he was in danger until Mahon's finger and thumb closed around his windpipe. He squeezed the way he was taught, forcing the boy's mouth to open and his tongue to unroll like a carpet. He slipped the bicycle spoke into his open mouth, and let it jab into the flesh. Let the boy taste his own blood. Let the terror take him. And then he told him that if he didn't smash Elton Flemyng's teeth in, he would come back. He would skewer him through the head and then go looking for his girl.

Mahon was saddened when he learned that the attack on Flemyng cost the boy his life. He noted the irony of him being skewered, though Mahon fancies that he would have made a cleaner job of it than those fools with the auger.

He moves swiftly. The cupboard fills with light as he opens the door and steps into the corridor. He has already counted how many steps this will take, which doors open outwards and which inwards. There are no cameras inside the building and the one that covers the car-park doesn't face the direction in which he will make his escape.

Five, six, seven...

The syringe sliding down his sleeve and into his left hand...

...eight, nine, ten...

The sharpened bicycle spoke emerging in his right hand as he passes the water cooler and the trio of blue plastic chairs...

...eleven, twelve...

Turning the handle on the surgery door and stepping into a square, brightly lit room.

Dr Malcolm looks around from his computer screen. Behind his spectacles his eyes widen in surprise. Then the syringe is in his neck and he makes a gurgling sound and slips down from his chair as if he is made of rags and stones.

Flemyng is in the chair, staring at the ceiling; black protective goggles cover his eyes and his mouth is propped open with plastic clamps. He does not move, just carries on listening to the hum of the radio, teeth bared in a rictus grimace. Mahon's face appears in his line of sight; his own teeth visible through the holes in his ruined skin. Flemyng chokes on his sudden, primal terror.

"You look like a skull," says Mahon, and pushes the bicycle

spoke through the gap between Flemyng's third and fourth ribs. He has wrapped one end in duct tape to serve as a handle of sorts but it offers little protection as he puts his weight behind it and pushes it all the way through Elton Flemyng and into the chair.

Flemyng tries to move. From his throat comes the sound of a frenzied, frightened swallowing.

"I'm Mahon," says his killer. "You might not know this but your little brother's dead. I took what was left of his head. I'm going to take yours now. Two isn't much of a collection, but it's a start. And I promise I'll have a lot more before the end."

Mahon pulls the cleaver from his pocket. The blood on the blade belongs to Tyrone Flemyng and he hopes that when the police examine Elton's neck, they will find forensic traces. He wants the Headhunters to know what to expect.

He brings the blade down as if chopping the head off a chicken. The cleaver chops into Flemyng's open mouth, digging as far as his jaw bone. In a spray of red, Mahon pulls the blade free. He chops down twice more, though skin and cartilage, bone and skull. When he is done, two thirds of Elton Flemyng's head is hanging to one side, clinging on by a flap of skin and hair. Mahon pulls it loose, as though tugging a dead plant from dry earth. He opens his jacket and removes the plastic bag he has tucked into his sleeve. He puts the head and the bag inside his coat, tucked up high, like a rugby ball.

Mahon does not look back. There are seventeen steps to the fire door and twelve down to the car park. He will be a street away before the alarm is raised.

As he moves, he has the decency to nod a quiet word of thanks to Blaylock for his part in bringing Flemyng here today. He would apologise for costing him his life but Mahon thinks that would be disingenuous and he doesn't like falsehoods.

As he emerges into the cold, blue morning, he feels a slight pressure in his armpit. Elton Flemyng's top teeth are gnawing against his skin. Mahon decides not to reposition him. He feels that Elton deserves the chance to fight back, even if it is too little and a lot too late.

11

There are two inmates seated at the plastic-topped table in the dining hall of HMP Bull Sands. One is a double murderer, sent down for life in 1981. His name is Ash. Before his incarceration he was a joiner. A father of two. A keen angler and committed football fan. Three and a half decades ago he caved his wife's head in when she told him she had no idea where he had put his car keys and suggested, quite reasonably, that he should hang them up on the hook by the door where they were supposed to go. He struck her seventeen times with the short, stout club he kept in his angling bag and which he had used the day before to end the suffering of a brown trout as it slithered and bucked in the wet grass. Forensic scientists later found the trout's scales inside the crumbled remains of his wife's compacted skull. When his neighbour came to investigate the screams, Ash killed her too. Then he slit his own throat. The police saved his life, then charged him with two murders. He's been in the prison system ever since, slowly moving through the different categorisations until landing here. He's due for release some time next year. He's fifty-nine now. A little portly. He's wearing a grey T-shirt, jeans and white trainers and there is a leather bracelet around his wrist, given to him by a twelve-year-old girl he has never met, but who calls him Grandpa. He is Owen's only friend inside.

"You're going to be nothing but dust by the time you get out," says Ash, looking angrily at the fresh bruise on Owen's face. "This can't carry on, mate. I've never pried, you know that's not my style. I know you're a target and everybody admires the way you refuse to let it break you. But how long will it be until people lose patience and you're fighting off a whole bloody prison on your own? Tell them, Owen. Whatever it is you're hiding, tell them."

"You're a good lad, Ash," says Owen, and smiles a little, as he realises the nonsense of the sentiment. He lets the smile fade quickly for fear of it causing fresh pain. There is a swelling around the hinge of his jaw and it hurts to chew, grin or talk above a whisper. Last night a house-breaker called Conroy came into his cell and said he'd heard Owen had been talking to coppers. He had an empty mug of tea in his hand and smashed it into Owen's face without further preamble. Owen took the first blow, hoping it would be the last. When Conroy continued to rain punches upon him, he retaliated. Conroy is in the hospital wing this morning with two cracked ribs and a fractured patella.

For four years, Owen has managed to survive by taking the beatings without complaint. He has fought back often enough for word to get around that he is no easy target. His time in Bull Sands has been easier than in the previous prisons where his tormentors had more influence. In Bull Sands, the man to fear was Elton Flemyng. He and his brothers made a deal with a very specialised group of individuals to take over the north east. He got his nickname because he celebrated his new alliance by having three crates of premium Russian vodka delivered to the wing and encouraging every inmate and warden to toast his success. He had the power to get himself a private room within Bull Sands, but he preferred company and comfort. One of those comforts was Will Blaylock, who he had transferred into his cell. Within a month, Will had smashed Elton's teeth out and been killed as an example – butchered by Flemyng's new associates to show what happened to people who cause problems.

Owen is exhausted. He feels like a dead plant that some fool continues to water. He has held one trump card up his sleeve for years but as his energy fades, so too does his resolve to keep fighting.

"They'll pay," says Ash, as if he has just had a wonderful idea. "If they'll hurt you time and again then there's no doubt they'll pay you for whatever it is you're holding back ..."

Owen is about to say something to lighten the mood when there is a sudden blaring alarm from the loudspeaker on the wall. All the men stand up instantly, expecting an announcement of a sudden inspection or roll-call. Instead, a reedy voice calls for all prisoners to remain in their cells and for all B-unit officers to attend the main gates immediately.

Owen looks up, bewildered. Officer Milne is holding a mobile to his ear and the colour has gone from his face.

"Escape?" asks Ash, under his breath. "Who was out and about last night?"

Owen says nothing. There have been plenty of occasions when inmates haven't returned to the prison. None has provoked such a reaction.

"What's going on?" asks Ash, as Officer Elwis bustles past. She's a small, buxom woman who gets up an hour earlier than she would like to in order to style her hair into a rockabilly qwuiff each day before her shift. She's one of the kinder faces on the wing.

"Not now, Ash," she says.

"Go on, Ma'am, just the bare bones..."

Officer Elwis gives the sigh of the eternally harassed and bends down low. "Flemyng's not coming back. Somebody got to him during his dental appointment. Cut his head off, from what we're hearing. Now, not a word. Off to your cells."

Owen feels like his heart is a bird trying to smash its way free of a cage. His vision slides a little, as though he is staring at the world through a porthole. He feels Ash's arm upon him, steadying him as they make their way back to their room. Ash deposits Owen on the bed and stands in front of him, face animated.

"Fuck!" he says, eyes gleaming. "Fuck, there's going to be blood on the walls, man. This is bad. Really bad."

Owen looks up. His legs do not feel as though they belong to him. He feels like the only man alive who knows what Flemyng's death means. He is talking before he even realises it. Once he begins, the secrets spill forth like water through crumbling brick.

"I'd have been dead like Flemyng four years ago if it wasn't for one bargaining chip, Ash. I've got dirt on somebody important. I've got their voice on a memory card, bragging about their lies. If I die, it goes public. So they hurt me. They push me as far as they can and tell me to give it up. But if I give it up, I'm dead."

"Owen, you can't fight forever ..."

"I'm so tired. I thought that maybe I could hold out a little longer but I don't think I can. I need your help, mate. I never ask for help but I need yours."

"Anything," says Ash, squatting down.

Owen looks deep into his friend's eyes. He has never allowed himself to trust anybody not connected to him by blood. He feels overcome by the sudden colossal need to be free.

"Get the memory stick for me and hide it somewhere I don't know about. Don't tell me where you put it. I can't know."

The lustre in Ash's face fades a little. "Owen, I can't do that. If you don't know they'll just hurt you until you can't get up."

"It's the only way I can think of not to break.. Please. You can get a cab from Boston and be back before roll-call. You'll be saving my life."

"Or taking it," says Ash, rubbing his nose and considering the proposition.

"It's just a taxi ride away," says Owen, and he feels drunk as he speaks. His mind is full of Elton Flemyng; this big, brutish man who seemed so damn untouchable. His eyes begin to prickle.

"I want to help..."

"The church at Randall House," Owen blurts out, and it feels as though the words shoot from his mouth like so much bile and blood. "My father was estates manager there. Lord Annsell allowed him to be buried there. In the chapel there's a loose flag, three pews from the cross on the left hand side. The memory stick's under there. Hide it. Keep it safe."

Ash's face changes. His features twist into something that might, in bad light, be taken as apology. And then he shakes his head and stands.

"You silly, silly bastard," he says, as though he is chastising a favoured pup who has eaten an expensive pair of shoes. "All those beatings? All that pain? You just needed a friend, didn't you? And I need some money to start again. I'm almost sorry about this. But I couldn't resist."

On the bed, Owen looks up through teary eyes. His face is cold. The tips of his fingers feel blue and numb.

"Ash?"

He shakes his head again and calmly walks out of the unlocked door. Owen is too dumbstruck to speak. A moment later, he returns, removing a slim mobile phone from a condom and wincing slightly. He peers at the screen and presses three buttons. A distant, soft ringing sound fills the small cell.

"I've got it," says Ash, flatly, into the receiver. "Location. He's spilled his guts."

It feels as though Owen's whole self is fragmenting. He imagines himself as a thing built of burned wood; a fragment on the softest breeze, swirling into nothingness in flakes and curls.

"He wants to talk to you," says Ash, handing over the mobile.

Owen's fingers shake as he takes the phone. It's cold against his burning cheek.

"You did well," says Doug Roper, and his voice is so smug that there should be oil running out of the receiver. "I almost admire you. But you broke. I win."

Owen can barely find the energy to hate. "I could have been lying," he says, but his voice is too weak for the threat to carry any weight.

"No, you're done. You're broken. And I'm bulletproof. Now, pack your bags and think about the future. I'm a man of my word and I said you could be paroled once you played ball. In a few days, you'll be on the outside with nothing between you and me but empty air."

Owen manages to say a name. "McAvoy ..."

"Don't you worry about him," says Roper, though his tone has become more harsh. "He'll be disappointed, of course. But suddenly you don't care about what happened to your little friend. You got it all wrong. You don't want to help him."

Owen had thought he stood a chance. That he could make it through his sentence then bring Roper down.

"Don't cry," says Roper, mockingly. "You've got so much to look forward to. I swear, your coming-out party will go down in history."

Owen drops the phone and slides onto the floor. He can barely hear Ash's voice as he seeks reassurances that the money will be deposited as promised.

On the dirty cord carpet, Owen presses his knuckles into his eyes hard enough to make them weep. He cannot let the mask slip now.

12

It's a cold and bright day, with a sharp wind blowing in off the sea bringing with it the smell of wet sand and rotting vegetation. Owen and McAvoy walk together up the narrow road from the dining hall to the administration blocks. Owen walks as though he is carrying a coffin on his back. He can feel something in the air; something he was witness to as a journalist and which he has grown to understand as a criminal. There is a tang to the breeze; the sense of a gale altering direction. Were he to try and describe it, he would talk about the sensation one experiences when a child is petting a strange dog, or that moment when the drunks in the taxi rank move from gentle name-calling to something more venomous. The whiff of violence.

"I'm sorry I don't have more to offer," says McAvoy. "But we're getting somewhere. We know that Will was acting on orders. This was all somebody else's plan. It's got links that go so high up the chain they don't even touch the street any more. If you were to testify we could move you. Put you somewhere safe."

Owen can barely hear him. Somewhere deep inside himself he remembers hating this man, feeling that he had abandoned him. Owen can barely find the enthusiasm for such hatred any more.

"I'm getting out, Aector," he says. "I can't be a part of it. Will got killed and we both know he didn't deserve it. Nobody deserved that death. But I can't be involved any more. I have to keep my head down."

Owen watches McAvoy struggle with his emotions. Even now, he wishes he could take some of the heartbreak out of the detective's eyes.

"I wanted to put things right," says McAvoy, at length. "I thought I had a chance to do that. Tell me, please, what else I can do. I can't carry this."

"I know how many burdens you carry, Aector," ," says Owen, with the tiniest twitch of a smile. ". There were times when I wanted you to wake up screaming, hating yourself for turning your back on me. Then I met you again and I realised you're already punishing yourself far more than I ever could. Go home to your wife. Talk about plants. Forget about me."

McAvoy is sweating, despite the breeze. He scans the horizon and as though he is hoping to see some kind of answer come charging in off the ocean. Owen feels sorry for him. Wants to tell him that very soon none of this will matter.

"You wanted my help," says McAvoy, beseechingly. "I know you did. The clues you gave me. The herbs..."

"None of it matters," says Owen, kicking at a loose stone. "We've both bled in each other's name. Let's not try to bleed more."

Their steps have taken them towards the prison exit. The main gates face out on to seemingly endless farmland; flat greens and browns stretching away.

"It feels like I'm seeing you out," says Owen. "Escorting you off my property like some country laird."

"Maybe one day you will," says McAvoy, though there is no optimism in his voice.

He stares intently and Owen has to look away. He feels a tug of memory. Finds himself remembering the day this man saved his life. He remembers holding the big, broad detective as he bled onto the forest floor. Remembers thinking of himself. Thinking of self-preservation. And then the call he made;

immortalizing the confession of an evil bastard who has tormented him ever since.

Roper was one of the first cops to arrive. He was white with fury. He already had a man in the dock for the crimes that Tony Halthwaite committed. He didn't need any heroic deed from a journalist or a holier-than-thou Detective Sergeant. As his team tried to make sense of the scene, as the paramedics tried to save McAvoy's life, as Tony Halthwaite screamed and blood pumped from the ragged wound to his groin, Roper took Owen to one side and demanded answers. Owen told him everything: that Halthwaite was a killer and McAvoy had risked his life to save him.

"*I don't give a fuck,*" Roper had hissed. "I hope the Jock bastard dies. This is my city. Mine! Do you know how many people I've put away just because they pissed me off? How many crimes we've chalked up as 'solved'? Do you know how many men are in the ground because they got in my fucking way? I'm Doug Fucking Roper, and you're going to die in more pain than you could imagine."

Owen recorded every word. It fed on to the memory card on the answerphone in his home. After Owen's arrest, he got word to his father. Told him to retrieve it and hide it. Told him that he would need a bargaining chip. When Owen was convicted, Roper's pets came for him. As they broke his bones, Owen heard Roper breathing heavily through a mobile phone held aloft in the cell doorway by one of the warders. He was enjoying the show. But he recognized his own words when Owen started repeating them from memory, mumbling Roper's own confession through bleeding lips.

For four years they tried to get Owen to tell them where the memory card was. He refused. Now he doesn't give a damn one way or another. He has heard the whispers about the men running organised crime on the inside and out. He has fitted the pieces together and he has learned that the man who has tormented him for so long has the power to make him, break him, or grind his bones to powder.

"I wish it had all been different," says McAvoy, putting his hand out to shake the small, damp fist of the man who was witness to what should have been his final breaths.

Owen takes his hand. "Not everything happens the way we want it to. But we can stack the deck. I know you won't let any of this drop, so I know this won't be the end of it."

McAvoy looks puzzled, as if trying to solve a cryptic crossword. Owen gives a little shake of his head. "There are so many bad people," says Owen. "I hope you stop some of them."

"I hope you never count yourself among their number," says McAvoy, releasing Owen's hand and half turning away.

"I'll send you a postcard from wherever I end up," says Owen, casting around for something to say that will relieve the numbness rubbing at his temples.

"I'll look forward to it."

They part without another word.

13

T he early evening brings with it a fine rain, almost a mist. The droplets seem to eddy , rolling with the cold breeze like birds on a choppy ocean.

A large car, parked in a disabled bay outside a brightly lit supermarket. Big halogen lamps battle with the blue and red neon of the shop sign.

Two men inside. One big and muscular, the other small and sickly-looking, his face lit by the glow of a laptop screen.

"He's sorry as Hell," says Michael Bee, looking at his phone. "Prick's shitting his pants. Should have thought of that before he cleaned out the Ponderosa."

"He says they warned him off."

"He's making enough money to buy some bigger balls."

"They don't mess around."

"They haven't done a thing to me, have they? If they think they can take my idea and make millions and give me no more than a piss-poor lump sum, they can fuck off."

"And Erskine?"

"He'll do what I tell him."

In the passenger seat of the 4x4, James Kinchie looks across at his companion. He gives an encouraging nod and returns his attention to the laptop on his knee. There are several different web pages open. A black memory stick pokes out of the USB slot. The stick is worth more than the car and the contents of the supermarket. So, too, is the website that is feeding it.

Kinchie looks again at the PayPal site he has been monitoring so intently. After a moment he punches the air.

"It's through. Final space filled."

"Everybody paid?"

"That's what I just said."

Bee turns to the younger man. "Don't get fucking smart."

Kinchie turns back to his computer screen and curses himself for allowing his brief moment of elation to override his good sense. He knows his companion's temper.

The James Kinchie who went to prison was nobody's idea of a criminal. He enjoyed cybercrime for the buzz. His world was one of secure chatrooms. His friends were people he had never met. He started syphoning off money from strangers' accounts simply because it was easy to do so. He never thought of himself as part of a criminal organisation. When his home was raided by officers from five different law enforcement agencies, he discovered that he had unwittingly become the administrator of a website used by some of the most lethal criminal organisations in the world. Prison did not suit Kinchie. He was small and feeble and had never had a fight in his life. He needed somebody imposing to be his protector. He found that in Michael Bee. In return, he became the larger man's property. When Kinchie revealed why he was inside, Bee saw an opportunity. Together, they could make a lot of money. They have been doing so ever since Bee was released. Now that Kinchie is out on licence, the possibilities seem almost endless.

The only obstacle is the fact that the business they established has been passed on to another organisation. Serious, well-dressed men with cold eyes and deep pockets contacted Bee and said they liked his style. They liked the idea and the operation. They wanted to buy it out, as if they were respectable venture capitalists instead of men with guns. They paid handsomely. Kinchie took umbrage, but he still took the money. The streaming sites were his idea. It was his expertise that allowed them to exist undetected – accessed only by prisoners with a phone and the code that would take them straight to the webpage. When Bee suggested they take their venture in a new direction, Kinchie did not argue. Sure, they had given up their rights to the business, but the reward was worth the risk. He left the morality of it to others and trusted Bee to keep them safe from repercussions.

"Lottie's got a new star," says Bee, his voice returning to normal. "Found her skipping school up on Hedon Road. Told her she could get her free hair extensions. I tell you t, that lass is worth her weight in gold. If Ronnie wasn't such an uptight cow she could have done all this for half the price but I suppose Lottie's a professional. Did I tell you she used to be an actress? She does real tears and everything, although I don't think I've met a girl who can't."

Kinchie isn't really listening. Bee sighs.

"I'm getting some cigarettes," he says, opening the car door. "If you notice I've gone, you can make a note of it on fucking Facebook."

Kinchie looks up as the car door slams. They are in the car park of the Tesco store in Beverley. He can't remember why. Bee said something about buying uniforms. He returned from a clothing store in the pretty market square with a carrier bag full of grey pleated skirts, white shirts, grey cardigans and school ties. Bee was pleased at how little the outfits had cost. It was in stark contrast to the masks which cost hundreds of pounds at the adult store. They were hideous to look at, vaguely reminiscent of animal heads. But they were beautifully made; each of the men who had worn one while participating in the live shows had commented on how comfortable and breathable they were. Kinchie just wishes he could claim back the VAT as a business expense.

"Now then," comes a voice as the driver's door swings open. "Don't be a silly twat."

Kinchie looks up, surprised at the change in tone. The man sliding into the driver's seat is in his mid-forties and has wiry grey hair and frameless glasses. He's holding a black gun and pointing it at Kinchie's head.

"Who are you?" he asks, in a voice that is part outrage and part surprise.

"You were told," says the man, and he turns the key in the ignition. "You were told to stop. Your friend's going to see what happens when we're disobeyed."

"Mike takes care of that stuff," blusters Kinchie. "I'm just the geek."

The man with the gun presses the locks as he eases the car forward. With a quick, deft motion, he jabs the barrel of the gun into Kinchie's temple. Kinchie protests for a moment but then the pain engulfs him, followed by unconsciousness. He slips down the window and blood runs from the wound on his skull to drip onto the keys of the laptop.

The man stops the car. Leans across and uses a stiletto blade to cut the ankle tag from Kinchie's leg. He winds the window down and drops it out. The back wheels crush it into the melting snow as he heads for the motorway. It will be a long drive, but the killer reckons the young man should try and enjoy it. It will be the last he ever makes.

14

It's a cold, clear night. The first crushed diamonds of a hard frost are sparkling on the grass verges and well-tended pavements of this pleasant, tree-lined street. While the sodium glow emanating from the streetlights is a gaudy, dirty yellow, the light that spills from the bay windows of these townhouses looks warm and inviting; throwing a soft radiance on black railings and neat gardens, expensive vehicles and terracotta pots that will be rich with flowers come spring.

Doug Roper sits in the passenger seat of an unremarkable hatchback and wonders if he would like living here. Whether he could buy a family home and fill it with little versions of himself. Wonders what the days would feel like, how he would resolve a boundary dispute with a neighbour in such a safe, reasonable world, whether he would lose his mind with the tedium of it all and simply shoot every single fucker he could see. He finds the whole vision almost funny.

Roper shakes it away. The thought of such a life is unsettling. This is what life should be. This.

"Like the car, boss?"

"It does the job."

"Torching or crushing down?"

"Sell it if you like. Give it to one of the girls."

"Fuck that. They get enough."

The stolen hatchback is blue but the streetlight overhead makes it look green, so that anybody who reports its presence will steer police in the wrong direction.

The interior of the car is thick with cigarette smoke. It gathers in clouds beneath the cheap upholstery of the roof. To Roper the effect is strangely beautiful. He wants to scoop the smoke into his hands and shape it like snow.. It turns his companion's black-coated mass into a drawing in smudged charcoal and if Roper were not so familiar with his associate Nestor's appearance, based on what he can see of him right now he would struggle to pick him out of a police line-up.

They sit in silence, enjoying the anticipation. These are the moments that Doug Roper likes best. Tonight he will be able to show himself, to work out his frustrations. Anonymity is crucial to his organisation and Roper takes pleasure in the knowledge that most of the people in his employ have no clue who he is or what he looks like. But from time to time he gets an opportunity to show his face, witnessed only by trusted underlings, and people who will soon be dead.

Roper is not an impulsive man. He has become something exceptional by virtue of being very clever and utterly merciless. Here, now, he would like to be stamping on Aector McAvoy's throat and setting fire to his wife, but he will resist such temptations until he's that he can trust his own judgement. He knows he is upset. Two of the Flemyng brothers are dead and he has no idea who killed them, or why. Roper hates to not know. Knowledge brings power, and power makes him feel the way he should. It took a man with vision to create The Headhunters. Doug Roper was that man. He had never expected to leave the police service. He was very valuable there. But when McAvoy and Owen Swainson cost him his career, Roper took it as a sign that he was destined for something more. He had long since come to the conclusion that most criminals have fewer brain cells than fingers. He understood that people are motivated primarily by fear and reward. He looked at the potential casualties of any turf war and came to the conclusion that breaking an outfit was a poor business decision. Better, he thought, to keep profitable organisations in place and merely skim off the top. Roper recruited. Contacts made during his time as a detective ensured he knew which criminals were biddable. He quietly set up a team of men with very special skills. And under his instructions, they took over drugs, prostitution and racketeering outfits in profitable territories up and down the country. "Another?" asks Nestor, offering the packet of pungent cigarettes.

Roper takes one. Lights it with his Ronson and enjoys the recollection of watching Owen's memory stick melt into a twist of blacknes.

"The other brother..." begins Nestor. "Safe?"

"They're over. It was only Elton who was holding it together. We'll let the rats fight it out among themselves and back the winner when it's done."

"And the other brother?"

Roper shrugs. "Fucked."

"They did pay," says Nestor, with a touch of reproach.

"Hard to reimburse a corpse," says Roper.

Despite his apparent disinterest, Roper prides himself that his operation is more than a protection racket for criminal organisations. Being linked to the Headhunters brings with it just not prestige, but access to considerable influence and assistance. Those who pay, can call upon Roper's organisation for help at any time. Elton Flemyng did that last summer. He made a call and barked out his demands for immediate retribution. His teeth had been smashed in by his cellmate and he wanted the little bastard killed. He wanted it to be a bad death. Roper's organisation has a key man at Bull Sands in its pocket and through deference to him, they decided not to have Blaylock executed within the prison grounds. Instead, their man Laurel was told to improvise, and he butchered Blaylock in a way that Roper could never have come up with. He demonstrated the benefits of being associated with the Headhunters.

Roper's influence ensured there were fewer questions asked than there should have been and Shaz Archer tidied up any loose ends. It all went as it should.

Roper almost enjoys the irony that the men who cost him his career are causing him headaches in his new organisation. Owen has been an irritant ever since that day in the woods, though Roper does admire the bastard's tenacity. Nothing he did could persuade Owen to give up the memory card. Roper couldn't kill him, in case, as he claimed, Owen had left instructions for the card to be sent to the authorities in the event of his death. And no amount of physical violence could persuade Owen to hand it over. Until now. Something has broken inside the stubborn bastard and Roper likes knowing that he has finally won. Earlier today he watched a computer screen as the memory card transformed beneath the flame of a lighter. With it went Roper's shame. He should never have made those threats or admitted the extent of his corruption. He has no doubt that should the authorities turn their attention to him they will quickly uncover the lies about his past and in time unearth the truth about him. They will learn that Doug Roper is a fiction. And they will discover that the men who back his operation and who made him rich while he was still a detective are more terrifying and brutal than he would ever claim to be.

"Here we go," says Nestor, the cigarette in his mouth moving as he speaks. He is looking at the screen of a military satellite phone. The symbols on the screen would be nonsense to any observer but him. He designed the code and he alone knows what the message means. He starts the car.

Roper and Nestor drive through the quiet streets in the direction of a small row of shops in a cosy neighbourhood near the river. It's all hipsters around here. People who recycle. Mums who don't wear make-up but still look good and dads who work as web designers. A community of people who visit delis and where children eat olives and pesto.

Third from the end of this little row of shops is a tea-room. It's cosy. The curtains are floral and the tea is served in cups with saucers. It specialises in bagels and is owned by a Ukrainian man who recently made some mistakes with his finances. The premises are valuable to the Headhunters because they come with a large, underground storage unit, dog out in Victorian times and roomy enough to secrete half a dozen tanks.

Roper and Nestor enter the property from the rear and open the hatch in the floor. There are eight steps down into the cool, dark mustiness of the subterranean vault and each one is patterned with blood.

"Good evening, Nigel," says Roper, standing away from the wall so as not to get dust on his coat. "And I believe this man is James Kinchie, yes? Hello, James."

The lad on the floor at Laurel's feet has two broken legs. Both wrists have also been snapped. He has little strength left in him but manages to raise his head as he hears his name.

Roper nods to Laurel, who steps back. "Don't go anywhere," says Roper. "There's work for you. I'm having him released Christmas eve. Hope that won't be a problem."

"No problem," says Laurel, and retreats into the quiet dark at the rear of the vault, leaning against a crate of vodka.

"You're a talented boy," says Roper, taking off his coat and handing it to Nestor without a word. "That video streaming. Great idea. More your thinking than Michael Bee's, I would say. I'm not bad on the old computer stuff myself, to be honest. We do a lot of business on sites that most of the law enforcement agencies don't even know exist. A webcam for perverts in prison? That was bloody wonderful. But you'll remember, James, that it doesn't belong to you any more. It belongs to my organisation. We gave you money to stop it and we made it bigger and better and more profitable. All you had to do in turn was stop running the shows and the girls and using that silly bloody farm in East Yorkshire."

Roper pinches his nose, as though exasperated at people's greed.

"You were compensated for what happened at the farm and the attention it brought you. You were asked to go away. You took the money and carried on like before. That was rude. We had to approach Mr Erskine direct. Laurel here had to get quite intimidating. But despite my best endeavours, a policeman started asking questions and now things are much harder to control. I'm a man who tries to see the positive in every situation but today, James... I'm not quite sure how I should be feeling, really, and that's quite a pisser for you. Because when I'm uncertain, I find it best to lose myself in physical exercise."

Nestor picks the lad up by his arms and drags him over to the wall. An old set of iron manacles has been punched deep into the old brickwork and two new, shiny chains hang from the rusty rings. Nestor snaps them shut around James's wrists, then reaches into his coat and hands Roper a curved implement with a hook at the end.

"Don't mind the blood at your feet," says Roper, conversationally. "I've used this place a lot. You might find this funny but until a week or so ago there was a copper chained up just where you're squatting. He's moved on now. New place, new pleasures. He's not the man he once was. Didn't even tell me to fuck myself as I hurt him. But keep that to yourself, eh? There'll be merry hell to pay if the missus finds out."

The implement in Roper's hand is an antique butcher's hook. Despite its age, there is no rust upon the metal. It was created to help abattoir workers and slaughtermen move large carcasses and the point of the hook is not particularly sharp. It was not designed to thrash human skin. But Roper is a man who spots potential.

He brings the weapon down, hard.

Takes comfort in the sounds of screaming, until the screaming ceases and there is just the thud, thud, thud, of metal on meat.

15

T he caretaker of the apartment block is a jittery, sixty-something man with acne scars so bad that McAvoy wonders if he occasionally loses his razor while shaving. His name is Alan and he is making so much noise with the ring of keys that he may as well be shaking a tambourine.

"It's okay, sir. Please. Let me."

"I've got it, I've got it," says Alan, and, his top row of false teeth slide forward in his mouth like a baking tray being pulled from an oven. He drops the keys as he raises his hand to his mouth, making a noise like an animal being trodden on. McAvoy gives an understanding nod and retrieves the keys.

It's mid-afternoon on a dry, blustery Thursday and on this estate of modern houses and tasteful flats, the men and women who seek entry to number 4B are in no mood for further delay.

"It's fine, sir. You've been a huge help."

Ben Neilsen steps forward and takes the caretaker gently by the forearm. He leads him towards the doorway of the neighbouring apartment block.

"I didn't know," says the caretaker, softly. "Do you think I'd have let it go on if I'd known?"

"Of course you didn't," says Ben. "Nobody's suggesting you did."

"She seems such a nice woman. Do you think she knows?"

"Leave it to us, sir."

McAvoy identifies the correct fob and holds it to the sensor on the key-pad. The door unlocks and he eases it open. He turns to the team of officers and tries to assemble his features into something encouraging. Looking at the unit, he realises he does not need to. They are ready for this. At the briefing, Pharaoh was honest with them all. She understood their desire to kick the living shit out of the men inside the apartment. She felt a similar urge herself. But a conviction was the important thing and they could not take any procedural risks. That being said, if anybody within the property looked like making a break for it, and their exit route should happen to lead down a flight of stairs, Pharaoh would not have a problem with them twisting an ankle or bumping their head a little on their way down the steps.

McAvoy breathes in. The lobby smells of other people's cooking. Something spicy perhaps. It did not take the Serious and Organised Unit long to put the operation together. With the assistance of the Technical Support Unit and a DCI from Vice, a warrant was signed that allowed technical staff to listen in to calls made on Michael Bee's landline. Forensic officers have visited each of the empty properties registered to his partner's portfolio. DC Sophie Kirkland and a PC seconded from community support have been trailing the former working girl identified by Ronnie as responsible for sourcing and grooming the pre-teens that Michael Bee has found so much more profitable than his stable of hookers.

McAvoy leads the way. There is no lift in the building and the adrenaline squeezing his lungs makes him feel light headed as he slogs up four flights of stairs. Flat 4B is straight ahead of him. To McAvoy's rear, a sergeant from Tactical Support is holding the long metal battering ram that the officers cheerfully refer to as a 'love hammer'. At McAvoy's nod, he plants himself in front of the door and waits for the order.

"In place, Guv," McAvoy whispers into the radio mic on the front of his stab-vest.

"Makes them sorry, Hector. Go, go, go."

The door smashes inwards and the sergeant stands aside to allow McAvoy and the team to thunder into the flat.

"Humberside Police," shouts McAvoy, pushing down the corridor and into an L-shaped living room. "This is a raid."

He stops short and feels Ben Neilsen thud into the back of him. Neilsen rights himself and takes two quick steps into the room. He, too, stops at what he sees.

The light in the room is unnatural. The curtains are drawn across the big rectangular windows and the room is lit by a large yellow spotlight. The sofa has been pushed back to create a space in front of the electric fire for an inflatable mattress. The bed is covered in soft toys. The pillows and quilt have a Hello Kitty cover. On the bed is an elderly man wearing a black leather mask. It has a zip for the mouth and mesh over the eye holes, a muzzle at the front and ears stitched on to give it the look of a dog's head. On the sofa sit three more men, naked except for bath-towels. Each wears a different mask. The man on the blow-up bed is trying to cover his nakedness without exposing the tiny pink feet of the girl he is trying to hide.

McAvoy absorbs the scene. Hears Pharaoh's voice through his earpiece and struggles to identify words in among the rage and static of his thoughts.

"Private party," says Michael Bee. He is sitting at the far end of the room, wearing headphones and looking at a laptop screen. "You can all get out of my fucking house."

Bee stands up. As he does so, he nudges the laptop and for an instant, McAvoy gets a glimpse of a dozen different men. They fill the screen like playing cards. Young, old, white, black, fat, thin. Each are in states of undress, and each has paid a premium to log on to this live streaming site and offer the perverts in the room suggestions on what to do. McAvoy feels faint. Sees animal faces and grey hair, bare feet and tiny eyes, and feels an anger that threatens to shatter him.

"You fucking sick..."

Behind him, McAvoy hears the words give way to a sound of pure, unpolluted rage.

He snaps to himself again. Sticks out an arm and stops Sophie Kirkland, who has produced her extendable baton and clearly plans to smash it down upon these men until there was nothing left.

Bee approaches the group of officers and blocks McAvoy's view of the small, pink feet with the chipped nail polish. "You can all fuck off." He stands in front of McAvoy, jaw locked. "She's just having a nice day with her uncles," he spits, spraying McAvoy's face. "She'll tell you as much."

McAvoy flicks his hand and the officers move forward; their body language speaking of their desperate wish to hurt the men in this room. As Bee protests, McAvoy's team start grabbing the men and pulling them towards the exit. All the while, McAvoy stands still, all but nose to nose with the bald, piggy-eyed man who made this happen.

McAvoy tries to look into the very soul of Michael Bee. Wants to understand the heart of this man who started off by streaming sex shows for prisoners. Then he pimped his girls to prisoners on day-release. Then he saw the profit in paedophiles. When Erskine cleaned out the Ponderosa, he started using his partner's empty houses for his shows. Today he's using his own home. He will do hard time, this time. He'll be on the wing with the nonces. He'll have to check every meal for piss and ground glass.

"Ask her," hisses Bee. "You won't make anything stick..."

From McAvoy's lapel comes a sudden burst of static. Then Trish Pharaoh's voice fills his world. She's watching the operation from the control room, looking into the apartment through the camera mounted on McAvoy's shoulder.

"Show me," she says, and McAvoy pushes past Bee. Ignores the man on the bed. Pulls down the quilt and looks into the brown eyes of a child. She's no more than eleven. The bruises on her chin are in the shape of fingers and thumb.

McAvoy feels a sudden shove in the back. He turns and Bee is squaring up to him, hands in fists. He's almost vibrating with his desire to do bloody violence.

"An ambulance," says McAvoy, softly, into his lapel. "Send the social worker up."

"She's fucking fine!" spits Bee. "It's a private party..."

"Hector, he's resisting arrest."

For a fraction of a heartbeat, McAvoy considers taking the swing. He could hit Bee just below the hinge of his jaw and knock his entire chin two inches sideways. But the girl on the bed does not need to see such things. Here, now, he just wants for none of this to have happened.

"Cuff him and read him his rights," says McAvoy, his eyes fixed on Bee's. "Then take him down the stairs. Be careful, though. He looks like he wants to run."

Ben Neilsen moves forward from the throng of officers hovering in the doorway. To the sound of curses and threats, the cuffs snap over Bee's meaty arms with a satisfying click. Ben hauls him upright and McAvoy steps in front of him, almost nose to nose. He's trembling, as if holding a pneumatic drill. He is holding his jaw so tight that the join between two molars is seamed with blood. He can taste it, rich and foul and energising: somehow magnetic.

"You're not even one of them," says McAvoy, in little more than a whisper. "You don't get off on kids. You did this for money. You put yourself in a room with people like this for money."

"Good money," snarls Bee, trying to sneer. "You want to know what we've made...?"

"We?" asks McAvoy, voice hoarse, throat closed. "You and Kinchie? Well, you won't get to spend your half, or his. Metropolitan Police found what was left of him on a railway line in Bermondsey. He was beaten to death with a meat hook. Pathologist says it took a long time. He wasn't a paedophile either. He was a kid who knew how to use computers and told you how the dark half of the internet worked. And you bought his soul. He's dead, but I hope to Christ that whatever happened to him in those last hours is a party compared to what your conscience does to you for the next twenty years."

McAvoy turns away and reaches out for something to lean on as the pressure in his head surges like the tide.

Ben drags Bee through the throng of officers milling in the doorway, straining to catch McAvoy's words. They look at the man who made this happen, and at McAvoy, the man who stopped it. He is too consumed by the crimson and dark to acknowledge the warmth in their eyes.

"You should have fucking hit him" says Pharaoh, in his ear.

McAvoy ignores her. Bends back down to the girl. He wants to stroke her blonde hair and show her that not all men are bad. He resists. He couldn't stand to see her flinch from his touch as if he were anything like those men.

"Arrest them," he says, to the team. "Arrest the lot of them."

There is the distant sound of a large man falling down a flight of stairs with his hands behind his back. None of the officers allow themselves to smile.

McAvoy surveys the men on the sofa. Their animal masks and naked torsos make them seem more ludicrous than monstrous.

"Don't let them change," he says. "Take them out just like that. And when you go past any reporters, say their names nice and clearly."

Pharaoh's dry laugh is loud enough for all to hear.

McAvoy does not join in. He is staring at nothing and listening to the sound of his own blood thundering against the inside of his skull like fists on stone.

16

On paper and above the door, the pub is called The Queen's Arms. To locals and the staff of HMP Bull Sands, it's Old Don's: named in honour of the publican who took it on in his seventies and died while changing a barrel of cask ale aged ninety-one. To the inmates, it has come to be known as The Starting Blocks. It is the first watering hole on the journey to freedom and could turn a profit just on the money spent by released prisoners. It sits two miles from the main gates of the jail and a further two miles from the outskirts of Mablethorpe. It's little more than a large cottage, with walls the colour of buttermilk and a sloping roof of shabby red tiles. Hanging baskets dangle from wrought-iron gutters and in autumn, peonies and gardenias collect in the wooden window-boxes. The wooden shutters that bookend the windows are painted a jolly red to match the front door and the blackboard by the porch proudly declares that the All-Day Breakfast is available from 12 noon until 2 p.m.

Owen feels the warming coolness of Guinness flood into his belly. He has not had a pint for four years. Prior to his incarceration, he was a borderline alcoholic. He was functioning. But he downed a bottle of half-decent Irish whiskey every couple of days and needed a couple of pints of the black by mid-morning. On the inside, accessing alcohol wasn't difficult but Owen needed his wits at their sharpest. In drink, he might have given in to the beatings and told Roper's underlings where to find the memory card. He endured the shivers and sweats and the crippling stabs of pain from his liver and kidneys and within a few weeks he no longer craved alcohol.

He craves it now.

It is Christmas Eve and Owen Swainson is a free man. The parole hearing was sudden. It took fewer than five minutes. At 3 p.m. the previous day he learned that he was to be released early for good behaviour. He was told to pack his possessions and report to the Sentence Management Unit. The goodbyes from the officers were cursory and professional. His few friends told him to be careful and to put as many miles as he could between himself and the prison.

Owen raises the beer to his lips again. Takes another pleasant, deep swallow. Puts the glass down on the bar and looks around him. Save for himself and the barman, the pub is completely deserted. He has time to examine it at his leisure. It's an attractive place; all wooden timbers and horse-brasses, varnished wood and old, spindle-limbed tables and stools. Owen would have spent a lot of time in here, back when he was a reporter. Could have happily spent a day in here with Tony Halthwaite, getting pissed and chatting up the bar staff and leaving with his notebook stuffed full of sellable tales. Owen has often wondered why he wasn't suspicious of Tony. He never made any attempt to hide his unpleasantness. He was cruel and venomous in the things he said about women and he would go to any lengths to sabotage his competitors. But he and Owen got on. Owen has spent a lot of difficult nights wondering what that says about him.

"Looks like that was a long time coming," says the barman, as he polishes the brass handle of a pump.

"Four years," says Owen.

"All up the road?"

"No. Harder time than that."

"Hope it hit the spot, then."

"After four years I'd drink battery acid if it came in a pint glass."

"We haven't got that one on the menu. I'll see if we can get it as a guest ale in the summer."

"I doubt I'll be here by then."

The statement has two meanings. Whatever happens, he'll be long gone by summer. The more important question is whether he will still be alive.

"You got plans, then?" asks the barman.

Owen considers him. He's late forties. Grey hair. Thin but muscly. Frameless glasses and white patches on his forearms where tattoos have been removed.

"I start work on January second," says Own. "Warehouse work."

"Near here?"

"North Yorkshire. Near Northallerton."

"Near the prison?"

"No doubt. They've got a good relationship with the company, apparently. Job came up, I was put in the hat. We'll see how it goes."

"Got a place to live?"

"Halfway house. Hostel, sort of thing."

"Should be okay."

"We'll see."

"What were you before, then? If you don't mind me asking."

"I was a journalist," says Owen, and it sounds like a guilty confession. "You gonna write a book, then? Jeffrey Archer did and it was a bestseller."

"I'm not sure anybody would be interested."

The barman looks at Owen with a half-smile.

"What did you do, then?"

Owen finishes his pint. Nods for another. "I did nothing when I should have done something. Four years seems quite lenient in comparison."

The barman starts pulling his pint. "I don't understand."

"No, you don't."

Owen half-turns away. The drink is making him feel a little blurry around the edges. He was panting when he pushed open the door and ordered his first drink. He walked briskly, almost at a jog, throwing endless glances over his shoulders while flat green fields stretched away in both directions like a blanket lain upon the earth. He helped work that land. He and Will. He wonders whether the cabbages will deliver the yield the foreman predicted. The cauliflower crop was clearly a disaster. As he walked from the prison gates he saw sheep chewing the leaves off the failed crop. He found himself laughing at the sight, a nervous, delirious noise. It looked as though the sheep, with their bushy white coats, were trying to camouflage themselves against the cauliflowers. It made him giggle, then the giggle gave way to tears. He has held himself together for so long that when the tears came they threatened to become a torrent. This wasn't how he imagined gaining his freedom. He always thought there would be somebody there to meet him, that he would be able to go to something that qualified as 'home. But he has no family left and nowhere to make for. He has only the money he earned on the inside which will pay for little more than a bus and a train and a few pints of Guinness. Survival has been his goal these past four years. Now the greater challenge begins. He knows he has only been freed so his murder can happen outside prison grounds. He doubts he will see the morning. He is drinking so he's numb when the bullet comes. Drinking so his death doesn't hurt.

"This one's on me," says the barman, and Owen turns back to him.

The barman is pointing a gun at Owen's chest. Owen looks into its barrel as though it were an eye. He refuses to let himself blink.

"I thought that Guinness was a bit amateurish," says Owen. "Gave yourself away a bit."

"Really? I haven't poured one in years. Thought I did okay."

"I've had worse," says Owen, raising his eyes and staring at the barman. "I've been to London."

"Aye, and I bet they charged you twice the price," he says, with a friendliness that seems incongruous in the circumstances.

"You sound northern," says Owen, cocking his head. "South Yorkshire?"

"Doncaster," comes the reply.

"Somebody has to be, eh?"

"So they say."

"And this is Roper, I presume," says Owen.

"Wouldn't like to say, mate. Names are dangerous things."

"He had me released just to have me killed."

"Your freedom for the memory card. That was the deal. He's got the card and you're free."

"Free to die."

"Don't get into semantics."

"Semantics? Unusual vocabulary for Doncaster."

"I heard you were from Hull, so don't get lippy."

They look at one another for a moment. Both men seem to find something to admire in one another.

"He's watching, isn't he?" says Owen. "Phone? CCTV?"

The barman shrugs. "He certainly seems to have been looking forward to this."

"So it's to be a bullet?" asks Owen, cautiously.

"I wish. No, this is going to take a while. I've a car outside. There's a farm building a couple of miles up the road. I've got a heater and a generator and there's nobody around. I can take my time with you. He seems very keen that you cry."

Owen nods. He inhales. Smells spilled beer and old wood, furniture polish and damp. Wonders if it would be best to make the man shoot him, if it would be a victory of sorts to force the man's hand and give himself a swift, painless end.

"Just like Will, eh?" asks Owen, and his lip twists as he says it.

"That was messy, I'll grant you. They just told me to be creative. He'd hurt somebody important, apparently."

"Did he suffer?"

"Not a lot," says the barman, sucking on his thoughts like a sweet. "I'm not a monster. I put a stiletto blade through his heart as soon as he turned around. It was always going to be a proper shitstorm of blood and gore and I couldn't deal with screaming and wriggling as well. You know men, we can't multitask."

Owen gives a tiny nod. He steps backwards as the barman flicks the gun and indicates that he should move.

"It was just because he attacked Elton Flemyng?"

The killer steps out from behind the bar and points Owen towards the door.

"The Flemyngs were part of the organisation. A message had to be sent."

"But Elton's dead. He had his head cut off at the dentist."

The barman smiles at that. "Yes. People are angry. I imagine I'll be getting a lot more work."

"Who does Roper think did that?" asks Owen.

"We have theories."

As Owen takes another step back, the barman puts a finger in his ear. Somebody is talking to him through a tiny ear-piece. Owen notices the pen sticking out of the pocket of the barman's black shirt. He smiles, staring straight into the camera lens.

"He's a clever lad, is Roper," says Owen, chattily, and waves. "Hi ,Doug. Still a cunt? Do you know much about him, mate? He's got vision. Got all sorts of ideas and schemes and really knows how to play people. Only lost out the once and that was when he stopped being a copper." He gestures again at the camera in the barman's lapel. "You in there, Doug? Bet you are. I've got to congratulate you. You did what you said. You got me out. I rather wish I'd believed you when you made that promise four years ago. But I still had things to lose then. I didn't want to die. Now?. I've got nothing left to protect."

"We're going for a little drive now," says the barman, cutting in.

"Is there another body in this building?" asks Owen, ignoring him. "Have you had this prick kill the landlord or is he just on holiday somewhere? If some punter walks by and sees the door open, you think they'll pop in and see what's going on? Will you have your monkey kill them too? How much death are you responsible for?"

"Move. Now."

"Fuck you," says Owen, coldly. He keeps his eyes on the barman's chest. "Like I said, I don't care about living any more. I'd be grateful for the peace and quiet of oblivion, truth be told. Thing is, Doug, I'm still pretty pissed off. I'm more than that, in fact. I'm fucking outraged, my friend. The man you put away is dead already. I'm somebody new. I'm all about revenge."

"I'll put a bullet in your kneecap," says the barman. "Move it."

"Will looked up to me," says Owen. "He needed somebody to tell about the big, scary man who put the knife in his mouth and told him to attack Elton Flemyng. He asked my advice. And I said to do as he'd been told."

"I won't tell you again..."

"I told him to do it because I knew the consequences of disobedience. I got on with Mitchell Spear. He was a useful contact. He told me a lot about the glory days of Francis Nock and his enforcer. I liked the sound of Mahon. He seemed like somebody with a code. Somebody who understood how things were supposed to be. And Mitchell was so easy to manipulate it was like he was made of plasticine. We both knew that if Mahon was alive, he'd come for Mitchell the second he was released. He'd have questions for him, and quite possibly a bullet. So Mitchell saved his own life and told Mahon about the pretty boy with fancy tattoos keeping Elton warm at night. Will Blaylock. He told Mahon about me, too. The man Roper fucked over who'd give anything to even the score."

"Stop talking..."

"Will did as he was told. Battered Flemyng's teeth in to give Mahon an opportunity to get to him. Will died for his part in it all and I'm sorry for that. But I don't feel terrible. Bad things happen to good people and I'm not even sure how good Will was. He fell in love with a hooker he met through a website, for God's sake. Hard to shed a tear for a man like that."

"I won't tell you again..."

"Getting free was an unexpected bonus. I was pretty content just having fucked with your organisation. But then I took a gamble. I decided to give you the memory card and see whether you would be true to your word. Do you think I didn't know that Ash was waiting for a chance to cash in on me? The man's a fucking idiot. It was still touch-and-go whether Roper would get me out but he's been true to his word – even if it is for his own reasons. What happens next is the interesting part. Now I see if I was right to believe in the moral code of a killer."

The barman takes a step forward, finger in his ear, wincing at whatever abuse he's receiving through the earpiece.

"You're still going to die," he hisses. "Slowly and painfully. I won't enjoy it but I'll do what I have to. My employer will give me instructions every step of the way. Some of it will turn my stomach. That's part of the job, unfortunately. Like I said, I'm not a monster ..."

"I am," says Mahon, from the doorway.

The shotgun has been sawed down to a little over a foot long and as Mahon pulls the trigger, the shot comes out more like a bomb than a bullet. The barman's upper body is transformed into a cloud of red and grey and what is left of him hurtles backwards to slam against the bar. His torso comes apart like boiled meat.

Owen's ears are ringing. He can feel his balance going. He wants to slide to his knees and then forward onto his face. He watches as a rain of blood drifts down to the carpet. Unsteadily, he turns to Mahon. Examines the man in whom he put his trust. He had no reason to believe that Mahon would come to his aid. But Owen pieced together a person he understood from the fragments of gangland folklore that Mitchell Spear shared with him. Above all, Owen identified a man with a code. He saw a way to win Mahon's loyalty. He told Spear that if Mahon ever came for him, he was to tell him how to get revenge on Elton Flemyng. Prisoners were allowed out for medical visits. Owen knew Mahon would not allow anybody else to kill Elton. He wanted the job for himself. Owen's way was perfect. He could have instructed Will to attack Elton himself but he needed to look like a bystander. He had to use all of his self-control not to grin with elation when Will told him about the huge man who sliced the roof of his mouth and ordered him to knock out Elton Flemyng's teeth. It meant that Mahon was alive; that Mitchell Spear had done what was asked of him; that Owen, perhaps, had a new and dangerous ally. Will's death was unfortunate but not unforeseen. It did not trouble Owen unduly. What little sympathy he had left bled away on the floor of his cell. He was sure that once outside, Roper would send his killers to end his life. He did not know whether Mahon would come to protect him. But it was better odds than he'd enjoyed in years.

Mahon approaches what is left of the barman. Prods him with his boot. Turns to Owen.

"I don't think he's getting up again."

Owen sees his lips moving but can barely hear a sound.

"It'll come back," says Mahon, gesturing at his ears. "I'm used to it."

"Thank you," says Owen, his ears suddenly clear. His voice sounds like a jet engine, startling him.

"You're welcome," says Mahon. "And thank you in return. Brave strategy."

"There was no other way. When all avenues of diplomacy are exhausted, you sometimes have to blow a man's head off."

"Mr Nock used to say that," Mahon says.

"I know," says Owen. "Mitchell told me."

"Mitchell told you a lot of things. I'm not sure I like you knowing about me. I'm quite enjoying being dead."

"I'm dead too. The second you're not there with a shotgun, somebody else will come and finish me. I can't go to this job in North Yorkshire. I can't go anywhere."

Mahon considers him. "What are you suggesting?"

"You already know."

"I'm not one for company."

"Neither am I. But we both want the same people dead. I could help. I can see you're not in your prime..."

"Not very wise words, bonny lad."

"You know the sense of what I'm saying. We could take Roper down. I know a copper who would give his fucking soul to see it through. He can be manoeuvred. I even managed to get a little bit of justice for Will. The copper's shut down the man who was pimping the girl he liked. But we don't want Roper in prison. We want him in pieces."

Mahon scratches at the tiny patch of skin visible between scarf and sunglasses. He exposes the gaping wound and Owen finds himself fascinated rather than repulsed. After a moment,

Mahon reaches into his jacket and removes a large silver cleaver.

"Quick test for you," he says, and slams the cleaver into the wood of the bar. "You think you can handle it?"

Owen walks forward and tugs the blade loose. He looks at what's left of the barman's corpse. Identifies what he thinks of as the neck. The half-moon of teeth, bone and twisted flesh comes away from the rest of the corpse with one slice of the cleaver.

"You'll need to bleed a little," says Mahon, nodding.

Owen rolls up his sleeve and makes a deal with a monster.

"Whatever it takes."

EPILOGUE

"No word?"

"Nothing."

"He may have staged the whole thing. May have had a plan..."

"The amount of blood, boss ..."

Pharaoh gives an understanding nod. She reaches out and puts her hand on McAvoy's. Hers seems unnaturally dark against his pale, freckled skin.

"I don't know if I helped him or made things worse. We still don't know who killed Will or if it was just an accident."

Pharaoh snorts a laugh and withdraws her hand. She has brought him to this little tea shop on Hull's Newland Avenue because it serves cake and scones on three-tier trays and the hot chocolate comes with enough marshmallows to build a cloud. She is sometimes accused of treating her dejected sergeant the same way as daughters when they are sad.

"You just stopped some very bad men from streaming live footage to a paedophilia ring. SOCA are chanting your name with delirium for the links we've found to organised crime and when I saw Ronnie she was wearing a business suit and looking a million dollars. The girl is doing okay. She's given us names and descriptions. We can't stop every crime but we can get justice, and you've done that and then some. Give yourself a break."

"But Owen started it all, boss. I wanted to get him peace. All that's happened is he's disappeared. Missing, presumed dead."

"You showed me the crimescene photos, Hector. Two types of blood. Brains and bone fragments. Evidence of a cleaver and a shotgun. SOCA are convinced it's all connected to what's happening to the Flemyng brothers."

McAvoy nods. The remaining brother is missing. Forensic scientists found evidence of a large, heavy cleaver having impacted with the floor of the apartment where he was hiding out in Long Benton; a trench in the centre of a sea of dried blood.

"I know there was more to it," says McAvoy. "What he said about Roper. He seemed to think he was more powerful than ever, that he was behind all the abuse he suffered in the last few years."

"All we can do is pass it up the chain. Try and relax. Eat your scone."

McAvoy manages a tight smile. Takes a bite of fruit scone, loaded with cream and jam. He manages to get some in his beard and on the tip of his nose. He blushes as he cleans himself up.

"It's true, is it?" asks McAvoy. "Archer's got the Drugs Squad?"

Pharaoh nods. "Acting Detective Superintendent. There's no arguing with her arrest record. I just wish she wasn't such a fucking cow."

McAvoy takes another bite and a swig of tea. Sitting on the metal chair at the round, wrought-iron table, surrounded by bunting and old newsprint, he seems more of an anachronism than ever, though where he would feel at home is difficult for Pharaoh to judge.

"Where are you spending New Year?" asks McAvoy. "We're going to be back in the house by tomorrow night. I'm sick of waiting. I've banged my head for long enough. You and the girls are very welcome."

Pharaoh considers him. Wonders whether she can endure

seeing Roisin's pert tits and flat belly as she plays the good little wife and shows Pharaoh's daughters what a cool mum looks like.

"Will there be roast potatoes?" she asks, closing one eye.

McAvoy nods. "I'm sure that can be arranged."

Pharaoh reaches across to take the last of McAvoy's scone.

"Who will I kiss at midnight?" she asks, through a mouthful of jam and cream.

McAvoy starts to cough on a crumb. She rolls her eyes as she rounds the table and bangs him on the back.

"You're an idiot," she says, affectionately, and pulls his beard as if ringing a bell.

"Thanks," he says, and his smile is a pleasing thing to behold.

The End

Printed in Great Britain
by Amazon

16222511R00088